Samuel French A

Nunsense.
The Mega-Musical Version

by Dan Goggin

‖SAMUEL FRENCH‖

Handwritten annotations:

URGENCY

↳ WE NEED TO GET NUNS
OUT OF FREEZE
IS VERY SCARY
TIME SOMETHIN
SUPER EXCITE
our number.
wanted to be

ask if bed moving
function as

we're all teachers at a
Catholic elementary school
we don't sass Revmo, she's BOSS
we live in FEAR.

clean group cutoffs

temptation w/
new tempo

FOR PRODUCTION INQUIRIES

UNITED STATES AND CANADA
info@concordtheatricals.com
1-866-979-0447
UNITED KINGDOM AND EUROPE
licensing@concordtheatricals.co.uk
020-7054-7200

Each title is subject to availability from Concord Theatricals Corp.,
depending upon country of performance. Please be aware that
NUNSENSE: THE MEGA-MUSICAL VERSION may not be licensed by
Concord Theatricals Corp. in your territory. Professional and amateur
producers should contact the nearest Concord Theatricals Corp. office
or licensing partner to verify availability.

This work is published by Samuel French, an imprint of Concord Theatricals Corp.

MUSIC AND THIRD-PARTY MATERIALS USE NOTE

IMPORTANT BILLING AND CREDIT REQUIREMENTS

THE COMPANY

STARRING

REVEREND MOTHER MARY REGINA *(Mother Superior)*
SISTER MARY HUBERT *(Mistress of Novices)*
SISTER ROBERT ANNE *(Streetwise nun from Brooklyn)*
SISTER MARY AMNESIA *(Nun who lost her memory)*
SISTER MARY LEO *(Novice who wants to be a ballerina)*

FEATURING

SISTER JULIA, CHILD OF GOD *(Convent Cook)*
SISTER MARY BRENDAN *(A teacher)*
SISTER MARY LUKE *(A teacher)*
SISTER MARY WILHELM *(Convent Nurse)*
FATHER VIRGIL *(Convent Chaplain)*
BROTHER TIMOTHY *(Stagehand)*

AND

CHORUS *(Nuns, Brothers, Priests, and Students)*

PLUS

FATHER (or **SISTER MARY**) **PATRICK** *(Musical Director/Conductor)*
SISTERS and/or **PRIESTS** and **BROTHERS** *(Musicians)*
SISTER MARY (or **BROTHER**) **SEBASTIAN** *(Stage Manager)*
SISTER MARY (or **BROTHER**) **DONALD** *(Asst. Stage Manager)*
SISTER MARY (or **BROTHER**) **MYOPIA** *(Spotlight operator)*

TIME

The Present

PLACE

Mount Saint Helen's School Auditorium

PRE-PRODUCTION NOTES
OR
WHAT YOU NEED TO KNOW BEFORE YOU START REHEARSALS!

In the "Large Cast" productions there are five major roles, and six featured roles, plus a chorus which can be as large or small as desired. The chorus can be made up of adults, teens, and/or children adults and teens playing priests, brothers, and nuns children as Mount Saint Helen's students. If young children are cast they should be used only in the tap dancing finale of Act One and the "Holier Than Thou" finale of Act Two. There is an option to bring them onstage when Sister Robert Anne does "veil tricks" at the beginning of Act Two. Because productions have various numbers of "Chorus" people, it is up to the director to decide which chorus members are used in various spots.

Depending on performer availability, several of the parts can be cast as men or women. For example if you wish to have more men in the cast, Sister Mary Brendan becomes Brother Brendan etc. Only the five main performers, Sister Wilhelm and Sister Julia definitely need to be played as nuns.

The stage directions are based on the original ground plan of the New York set designed by Barry Axtell. (The ground plan is included with this script.) If other designs are used, the director needs to adjust stage directions accordingly.

In the original production the tap challenge was performed by Sisters Hubert, Leo, Amnesia and Robert Anne. In the "large cast" the best tap dancers, principals and/or chorus, should be used. (Rev. Mother and Sister Julia cannot be a part of the tap challenge.)

MUSICAL NUMBERS

ACT ONE

Overture . . . . Orchestra
Veni Creator Spiritus . . . . Sr. Robert Anne & All
Nunsense is Habit Forming . . . . All
A Difficult Transition . . . . Alll
Benedicite . . . . Srs. Leo & Hubert
The Biggest Ain't the Best . . . . Srs. Hubert & Leo
Another Surprise . . . . Sr. Robert Anne
Playing Second Fiddle . . . . Sr. Robert Anne
Second Fiddle Conclusion . . . . Sr. Robert Anne
So You Want to Be a Nun . . . . Sr. Amnesia & Sr. Annette
Mock Fifties . . . . Srs. Leo, Robert Anne, Luke & Brendan
A Good Cause . . . . Srs. Brendan, Wilhelm, Virgil, Julia, Luke,
                                                        Hubert & Rev. Mother
Turn Up the Spotlight . . . . Rev. Mother
Lilacs Bring Back Memories . . . . Srs. Leo, Hubert, Amnesia
                                                        & Rev. Mother
Turn Off That Spotlight / Tackle That Temptation . . . . All

ACT TWO

Growing Up Catholic . . . . Srs. Robert Anne & Chorus Nuns
Clean Out the Freezer . . . . Chorus
Just a Coupl'a Sisters . . . . Rev. Mother & Sr. Hubert
Second Fiddle (Reprise) . . . . Sr. Robert Anne
I Just Want To Be a Star . . . . Sr. Robert Anne
The Drive-In . . . . Srs. Leo, Amnesia & Robert Anne
I Could Have Gone to Nashville . . . . Sr. Amnesia
Gloria in Excelsis Deo . . . . All
Holier Than Thou . . . . Sr. Hubert & All
Nunsense (Reprise) . . . . All

I₁   *[MUSIC NO. 00: "OVERTURE"]*

(The musicians enter. They are part of the religious community and are dressed in their religious garb. They begin playing the overture. **SRS. HUBERT, ROBERT ANNE, LEO, LUKE, BRENDAN,** *and a select number of* **CHORUS MEMBERS** *come into the auditorium and begin visiting with members of the audience. In general, they warm up the crowd. After about three or four minutes* **SR. ROBERT ANNE** *goes up on the steps leading to the stage.)*

SR. ROBERT ANNE. Ladies and gentlemen, may I have your attention please. Reverend Mother is on her way over here and I thought maybe you would all do me a big favor and help put her in a good mood. 'Cause believe me, there is nothing worse than a crabby Reverend Mother. What I'd like you to do is, when she arrives give her the Mount Saint Helen's cheer. If you don't remember it, here's how it goes. *(raising her fist in the air)* Woo! Woo! Woo!. Let's try it on the count of three. One, two, three! Woo! Woo! Woo! That's great. Now do we have any whistlers in the audience?

*(***BR. TIMOTHY** *enters right followed by* **REV. MOTHER.***)*

BR. TIMOTHY. Here she is folks. Our own Reverend Mother, Sister Mary Regina!

*(***REV. MOTHER** *comes to the front of the stage acknowledging applause. She then surveys the stage and notices a poster of Marilyn Monroe in a bathing suit. She is visibly upset and orders* **BR. TIMOTHY** *to get a drape off the easel announcing the performance. She goes up and pins the drape to Marilyn while* **BR. TIMOTHY** *takes the easel offstage left.* **REV. MOTHER** *rings a bell summoning the cast members in the audience to the stage.*

come up during processional

NERVOUS EXCITEMENT

Bell enter to position & hands in pockets

They come up immediately as **REV. MOTHER** *conducts the band. On stage* **SR. HUBERT** *sits at the lunch counter.* **SR. ROBERT ANNE** *sits on the stool next to the juke box.* **SR. LEO** *sits on the bed.* **SRS. BRENDAN &** **LUKE** *are standing/sitting at various parts of the stage to "fill out the stage picture." The* **CHORUS MEMBERS** *exit left and/or right.* **REV. MOTHER** *conducts the band faster and faster to the end of the "Overture.")*

SR. HUBERT. Let's hear it for the Mount Saint Helen's Band!

REV. MOTHER. *(taking center stage)* Are we ready to begin?

SR. HUBERT. Reverend Mother, where's Sister Amnesia?

REV. MOTHER. *(looking around)* Sister…Sister Amnesia? *(***SR. AMNESIA** *peeks out stage left.)* Oh, there she is. Come out, Sister. It's okay. They're all friends.

*(***REV. MOTHER** *leads* **SR. AMNESIA** *to the bed and puts her next to* **SR. LEO** *and pats her on the head.)*

REV. MOTHER. *(to audience)* She's a little nervous. *(While walking back to center stage she adds:)* She's a big mess is what she is! *(to* **SR. HUBERT***)* Now, are we ready?

*(***SR. HUBERT** *nods yes.)*

*(***REV. MOTHER** *clicks her clicker to summon the spotlight operator.)*

REV. MOTHER. *(If audience laughs:)* Brings back memories, huh?

(If small or no laughs:) Not many Catholics here tonight (today)!

Alright, may I have some light please?

(The spotlight comes on in the wrong place then moves erratically around the stage as **REV. MOTHER** *hollers directions trying to get the light on her face. Finally the light is right.)*

REV. MOTHER. That's Sister Mary (or Brother) Myopia — our archery instructor.

Good evening, friends.

→ afternoon for matinee

(She pauses as all on stage conduct the audience in responding, "Good evening, Sister.") conduct audience

Oh, we sure can train 'em, can't we Hubert? On behalf of the Little Sisters of Hoboken, I'd like to say: "Welcome to the theatre of Mount Saint Helen's School!" And may I extend our gratitude to each and everyone of you for coming here to participate in our fund-raising activities. Now, before we begin, I'd like to clear up what seems to be some confusion about the set here. You see, our eighth graders are putting on the musical, "Vaseline" and I gave –

SR. HUBERT. *(rushing over to* **REV. MOTHER** *and speaking quietly)* It's "Grease."

REV. MOTHER. What?

SR. HUBERT. *(louder)* It's "Grease!"

REV. MOTHER. *(looking at her white collar)* Where?

SR. HUBERT. *(turning* **REV. MOTHER** *around to see the set logo)* "Grease!"

REV. MOTHER. Oh! – It's "Grease." Who knew?

*(**SR. HUBERT** goes back to her seat and as she is walking waves her hand over her head indicating that **REV. MOTHER** is clueless.)*

Well, anyway, I promised the children that we wouldn't disturb their handiwork during our benefit and so that's why things may seem a bit incongruous at times. Now, we have a wonderful introductory song, but before we begin the festivities, let us ask the Lord to bless us in our endeavors. Sister, *(indicating* **SR. ROBERT ANNE***)* if you will.

[MUSIC NO. 02: "VENI CREATOR SPIRITUS"]

#9

SR. ROBERT ANNE.

VENI CREATOR SPIRITUS.

X4 – between Kayla &...

ALL.

MENTES TUORUM VISITA.

Keep vol up

IMPLE SUPERNA GRATIA.

QUAE TU CREASTI PECTORA.

DS

Super wacky conga

#13.5

[MUSIC NO. 03: "NUNSENSE IS HABIT-FORMING"]

ALL.

SOME FOLKS THINK OF CONVENTS
AS THE PLACES WHERE WE PRAY.
BUT LET US TELL YOU CONVENTS
ARE MUCH MORE THAN THAT TODAY.
WE'RE DEDICATED PEOPLE
BUT WE LIKE TO HAVE OUR FUN.

REV. MOTHER.

WE'RE HERE TONIGHT (TODAY) TO SHARE WITH YOU
THE HUMOR OF THE NUN!

ALL.

NUNSENSE IS HABIT-FORMING
LET US TELL YOU WHY.

REV. MOTHER.

WHEN A SISTER GETS APPLAUSE,
IT'S A SPECIAL "HIGH."

ALL.

THERE IS NOTHING WE CAN DO
ONCE WE GET A LAUGH OR TWO.
IT'S SOMETHING WE CANNOT CONTROL
ONCE WE'RE ON A ROLL!

SR. ROBERT ANNE.

look @ ppl talking

HAVE YOU HEARD THE ONE ABOUT THE TRAVELING SALES
   NUN
WHO REALLY DREW A CROWD?
IT SEEMS THIS FARMER HAD A HORSE
RATHER WELL-ENDOWED –

REV. MOTHER.

SISTER! NUNSENSE MAY BE HABIT-FORMING
BUT LET'S DRAW THE LINE!

SR. HUBERT.

CUT THE CHEAP SHOTS! WHY BE COMMON?

REV. MOTHER.

WE CAN BE DIVINE!

ALL.

EVERYBODY'S HERE SO LET'S TELL 'EM WHO WE ARE:

REV. MOTHER.

look @ ppl
talking

THIS IS SISTER ROBERT ANNE
SHE SINGS AND DRIVES THE CAR.
SISTER MARY AMNESIA
DOESN'T KNOW HER REAL NAME.

ALL BUT SR. AMNESIA.

A CRUCIFIX FELL ON HER HEAD.
HER MEMORY'S GONE.

ALL.

WHAT A SHAME!   5 6 7 & 8

SR. ROBERT ANNE.

SISTER HUBERT IS OUR NOVICE MISTRESS –
SECOND IN COMMAND.

SR. LEO.

SISTER LUKE AND SISTER BRENDAN
ARE HERE TO LEND A HAND.

SR. HUBERT.

SISTER LEO IS THE YOUNGEST,
AS A NOVICE, SHE'S BRAND NEW.

REV. MOTHER.

AND I'M YOUR REVEREND MOTHER
SISTER MARY REGINA, THAT'S WHO!

ALL.

NUNSENSE IS HABIT-FORMING,
THAT'S WHAT PEOPLE SAY.
WE'RE HERE TO PROVE THAT NUNS ARE FUN,
PERHAPS A BIT RISQUE.   →down
WE STILL WEAR OUR HABITS
TO RETAIN OUR MAGIC SPELL.

ALL.

THOUGH WE'RE ON OUR WAY TO HEAVEN,
WE'RE HERE TO RAISE SOME HELL!

REV. MOTHER.

SELL IT, GIRLS!

(At this point the entire chorus of nuns comes on stage and forms a giant chorus line.)

ALL. [handwritten: step L]

NUNSENSE IS HABIT-FORMING,
THAT'S THE REASON WE ARE
UP HERE ON THE STAGE TONIGHT (TODAY)
HOPING YOU'LL AGREE.

[left margin handwritten: #5, sling the poo off feet, sharp umph, add shoulders, Back to 13.5]

REV. MOTHER, SRS. ROBERT ANNE, & HUBERT.
NUNSENSE IS HABIT-FORMING, [handwritten: step R first]

SRS. AMNESIA, LUKE, BRENDAN & LEO.
(overlappping with above) AND WERE HOOKED

ALL.

AND ALL WE KNOW IS:
WE JUST CAN'T KICK IT, [handwritten: → to R]
THOUGH SOME FOLKS MAY PICKET,
WE JUST CAN'T KICK THIS NUNSENSE.
SO ON WITH THE SHOW!

[left margin handwritten: 15 COUNTS, BREATH ON LAST NOTE, keep hands up on I]

*(Quick blackout, lights up. All of the **SISTERS** are congratulating each other as **SRS. ROBERT ANNE,** **AMNESIA, LEO,** exit stage right. **SRS. LUKE** & **BRENDAN** exit left. The **CHORUS** exits at points nearest to where they ended the song. **REV. MOTHER** is center. **SR. HUBERT** stands at her right.)*

[left margin handwritten in red: more excitement]

[left margin handwritten: Iii]

REV. MOTHER. Oh, thank you. Thank you so very much. And how about a hand for our wonderful Mt. Saint Helen's chorus! *(She leads applause.)* Now, just in case there is anyone here who hasn't heard what our little fund-raiser is all about – we've had a small disaster back at the convent. You see, a short time ago, our cook, Sister Julia – *(both cross themselves)* Child of God, served some vichyssoise soup and nearly every sister died instantly of botulism!

SR. HUBERT. It was kind of like the last supper! *(She laughs at her joke.)* That's a little convent humor!

*(**REV. MOTHER** is not amused at **SR. HUBERT**'s stealing the spotlight.)*

REV. MOTHER. Why, we wouldn't be here now if it hadn't been for the fact that we were off playing bingo with some Maryknoll Sisters. *(to* **SR. HUBERT***)* What a bunch of cut-throats they turned out to be, huh?

SR. HUBERT. *(rather excitedly)* I still say their Mother Superior cheated when she didn't call B-15! I know she had it.

REV. MOTHER. Now, calm down, Sister. Lord knows, she's not pretty, but she doesn't cheat.

SR. HUBERT. She does, too. B-15 – I saw her slip it right up her sleeve. It was all I needed to win.

But that's alright! 'Cause God don't like ugly!

REV. MOTHER. *(to audience)* The point is when we got back to the convent we found fifty-two of our sisters lying face down in that soup!

SR. HUBERT. Now, we had no idea what to do so we all began praying for guidance.

REV. MOTHER. Then I had a vision. It was either Saint Catherine of Siena or Saint Thomas Aquinas in drag. *(pause)* I never could tell 'em apart – *(pause)* Never have seen 'em together! Anyway, I was instructed to start a greeting card company to raise funds. Well, of course I did – and it was a huge success!

SR. HUBERT. So we took the money and buried 48 of the 52 dead sisters and then Reverend Mother bought a Plasma TV for the convent. *(pause)* Personally, I thought we should have buried all of the sisters before we bought the Plasma TV, but as Mistress of Novices I'm only "number two" around here so one tries hard not to question Reverend Mother.

REV. MOTHER. *(getting very irritated)* And one will try –

BOTH. – Harder in the future!

REV. MOTHER. That's right, dear!

(**REV. MOTHER** *points the index fingers of both hands at* **SR. HUBERT***'s face and makes a "ZZZZZZTT" sound as if to zap her.)*

The worst part is, we had to put the last four sisters in the freezer!

SR. HUBERT. And the Ben & Jerry's ain't tasted the same since!

REV. MOTHER. That's why we're putting on this little show. We've got to raise enough money to bury those last four dead sisters!

SR. HUBERT. We hope you'll forgive the limitations put on us by the loss of so many of our sisters, but if they hadn't died, we wouldn't have to bury them, and then there wouldn't be this little show in the first place.

REV. MOTHER. *(to* **SR. HUBERT***)* But they did, we have to, and there is, so there you are!

(Using the index fingers of both hands and pointing them at each others faces they "zap" each other in unison: "ZZZZZZTT." Then **REV. MOTHER** *continues to talk to the audience:)*

Now, about a week ago I held tryouts for our show and I picked the sisters whom I felt we're the very best – of what's left of us – and I asked each one of them to prepare something that best displayed her talent.

SR. HUBERT. But first, I thought you might be interested in knowing some of the history of the Little Sisters of Hoboken and that's what our next song is all about.

REV. MOTHER. *(sarcastically)* Thank-you, Hubert.

SR. HUBERT. Don't mention it.

*(***SR. HUBERT*** exits stage right and immediately returns with* **SRS. LEO, AMNESIA, ROBERT ANNE, LUKE** *and* **BRENDAN***, and some or all of the* **CHORUS** *[excluding the students].* **REV. MOTHER** *continues with the audience:)*

REV. MOTHER. You see, we started out running a leper colony. Oh, I know some of you probably think that's a bit distasteful, but all the other causes were taken! You see, it all began when we –

(The cast is in place but something is wrong and **SR. LEO** *interrupts* **REV. MOTHER** *by whispering something in her ear. Without another word,* **REV. MOTHER** *takes* **SR. AMNESIA** *by the shoulders and moves her to the proper position.* **SR. LEO** *goes to her spot.)*

(to **SR. AMNESIA***)* Wasn't that a fun trip?!

*(***SR. AMNESIA** *nods.)*

Alright, are we ready? Father (or Sister Mary) Patrick, let's do it!

FR. PATRICK. Five, six, seven, eight!

[MUSIC NO. 04: "A DIFFICULT TRANSITION"]

ALL.

AVE MARIA! IT'S SO HEAVENLY TO BE A
MEMBER OF A GROUP THAT'S PUTTIN' ON A SHOW!

SR. ROBERT ANNE.

IT'S GREAT!

ALL.

ALTHOUGH IT IS A DIFFICULT TRANSITION
FOR WE STARTED OFF AS MISSIONARIES
WHICH, OF COURSE, IS OBVIOUSLY
MUCH MORE APROPOS.

SR. AMNESIA.

BUT THEIR MISSION GOT IN TROUBLE.   step touch

SR. LEO.

AND THAT BURST THEIR HOLY BUBBLE.

REV. MOTHER.

WE WERE CAUGHT IN AM IMBROGLIO,

SR. HUBERT.

AND WE FINALLY HAD TO GO.

ALL.

SO WE HOPE YOU'LL UNDERSTAND
IF WE'RE NOT ABSOLUTELY GRAND.

SRS. AMNESIA & LEO.

FOR WE FEEL A LITTLE QUEASY,

ALL.

WE'RE UNEASY IN THIS SHOW.   down 7
                                    pray 1   #2

REV. MOTHER. Let me start from the beginning. Now pay attention! We're going to give you the history of our order and you're going to be quizzed on it afterward.

FILLED WITH GREAT ANXIETY
SISTER HUBERT SAILED WITH ME
AND SISTER ROBERT ANNE
TO A LAND OF UNKNOWN CIRCUMSTANCE.

WE REACHED OUR DESTINATION
WITH A BIT OF TREPIDATION   *stop*
FOR WE'D COME TO ORDER LEPERS
BACK TO WORK IN SOUTHERN FRANCE.

stop on 7

SR. ROBERT ANNE.

NO!

SRS. HUBERT & BRENDAN.

NO!

SRS. LEO & LUKE.

NO!

ALL.

NO!

REV. MOTHER. Oh, no! That's not right! We'd come to join an order working with lepers on an island south of France. That's it!

ALL.

more fast

EACH OF US, AS BEST WE COULD,
CUT A TREE AND CHOPPED SOME WOOD
WHICH THEN WAS USED IN BUILDING
HUMBLE HUTS FOR QUARANTINE.

WHEN SISTER MARK YVONNE
HAD FINISHED UP THE PORTA-JOHN,
WE ALL SAT DOWN AND WAITED
FOR THE FIRST OF THOSE UNCLEAN.

REV. MOTHER. And they came from everywhere!

SR. ROBERT ANNE.

LOTS OF DICTION

THERE WERE HOTTENTOTS WITH ROTTEN TOTS
IN BASKETS ON EACH MOTHER'S HEAD.

SRS. AMNESIA & LEO.

> AND ZULUS, THEY CONCLUDED
> NEVER UNDERSTOOD A THING THEY SAID.

SR. HUBERT.

> UBANGIS WHO WERE GANGING UP
> ON NATIVES WHO WERE BEING FED.

SR. ROBERT ANNE.

> AND SWAZI WHO WERE GOOSING
> ALL THE BUSHMEN IN THE LINE AHEAD.

ALL.

> IT WAS DREADFUL!
>
> THE PYGMIES HAD THEIR NOSES
> STUCK IN EVERYBODY'S BUS'NESS
> WHILE WATUSIS HAD THEIR BUS'NESS
> STUCK IN EVERYBODY'S NOSE.
>
> BUT THE TRUTH OF THE MATTER,
> IF YOU REALLY WANT TO KNOW,
> WAS THAT EVERYBODY'S BUS'NESS
> WAS ABOUT TO DECOMPOSE.

circle arms on exit

REV. MOTHER. *start steps*

> HUBERT, ROBERT ANNE, AND I
> ARE LUCKY THAT WE'RE STILL ALIVE
> FOR SISTERS WENT TO PIECES
> AT A DEVASTATING RATE.
>
> WHEN A NOVICE SPILLED HER FOOD,
> AT FIRST, WE THOUGHT HER RATHER CRUDE
> TILL WE REALIZED HER HAND
> WAS ON THE FLOOR WITH HER FORK AND HER PLATE!

ALL. Wait!

REV. MOTHER. There's more!

SR. HUBERT.

> THE PROTESTANTS, IT SEEMS,
> HAD SET OUT TO WRECK OUR DREAMS.

ALL.

> WE HAD HUMBLE HUTS
> WHILE THEY BUILT LEPER CONDOS-BY-THE-SEA.

REV. MOTHER.

> COMPETING FOR EACH LEPER
> PUT OUR MISSION WORK IN JEOPARDY.
> SO WE DEVISED A PLAN
> TO AVOID CATASTROPHE.

SR. HUBERT.

> WE CHALLENGED THEM TO RACE
> 'CAUSE WE THOUGHT WE'D TRUMP THEIR ACE
> IN THE HUNDRED METER DASH
> WHEN WE ENTERED SISTER ROSE.

SR. ROBERT ANNE.

> BUT AS SHE WAS VICT'RY-BOUND,
> HER SCHNOZ FELL ON THE GROUND.

ALL.

> IF IT HADN'T FALLEN OFF
> SHE'D HAVE WON IT BY A NOSE!

REV. MOTHER.

> POOR ROSE!

ALL.

> OOOOHHHHHH…BUMMER!

REV. MOTHER.

> HUBERT, ROBERT ANNE, AND I
> HAD MANAGED ONCE MORE TO SURVIVE
> BUT THIS TIME WE KNEW
> WE WERE IN A TRULY HOPELESS SPOT.

SR. ROBERT ANNE.

> SO WE PACKED UP WHAT WAS LEFT,
> FEELING TOTALLY BEREFT,
> AND GOT OUT WHILE THE GOING
> WAS STILL ABLE TO BE GOT.

REV. MOTHER, SRS. ROBERT ANNE & HUBERT.

> WE CAME BACK HOME TO HOBOKEN
> BUT WITH SPIRITS SO BROKEN
> NO ONE REALLY KNEW
> IF WE'D PULL THROUGH. → keep swaying thru 8

SRS. AMNESIA, LUKE, BRENDAN & LEO.

> THEN REV'REND MOTHER PRAYED
> THERE WOULD BE A NEW CRUSADE.

ALL.

> AND WE WERE DOING GREAT
> TILL SISTER JULIA MADE THAT STEW!
> *(eyes heavenward)* MON DIEU!

> AVE MARIA, IT'S SO HEAVENLY TO BE A

REV. MOTHER.   *hands in pocket*

> MOTHER!

ALL WOMEN.

> SISTER!

ALL MEN.

> BROTHER!

ALL.

> MAKING A DEBUT IN FRONT OF YOU.
> IT'S A DIFFICULT TRANSITION
> FOR THE MISSIONER'S POSITION
> WAS UP TILL NOW THE ONLY ONE WE KNEW,
> IT'S SAD, BUT TRUE.

> SO WE HOPE YOU'LL UNDERSTAND
> IF WE'RE NOT ABSOLUTELY GRAND.
> BUT WE WILL DO OUR BEST
> TO SEE THAT YOU'RE IMPRESSED.   *hands @ sides*
> WE HOPE WE'LL PASS THE TEST. *hands @ sides ✓ on 8*
> NOW THE REST IS UP TO YOU! AMEN! *→ to pray on 5 (someone will hand onstage)*
> *(Quick blackout. Lights up.)*
> *(grab mic SL)*

X US of everyone to grab mic SL

> *(**REV. MOTHER** & **SR. HUBERT** stay toward center stage *go to DS stairs*
> as **SR. LEO** exits left. **OTHERS** leave by exit nearest. **SR.**
> **ROBERT ANNE** exits right followed by **SR. AMNESIA**.)*

Iiii

SR. HUBERT. *(seeing **SR. AMNESIA** leaving)* Sister Amnesia.
Sister Amnesia, where are you going?

SR. AMNESIA. *(pointing to the exit)* I was just going with what's-
her-veil.

SR. HUBERT. But aren't you in charge of the quiz?

SR. AMNESIA. Oh, I forgot.

> *(**SR. AMNESIA** goes to the locker to get her ruler.)*

SR. HUBERT. I just can't seem to get through to her, Reverend Mother.

REV. MOTHER. I know. I keep hoping if she remembers who she is, we'll discover she belongs to the Franciscans.

*(***REV. MOTHER*** *exits left as* **SR. AMNESIA** *comes center.)*

SR. HUBERT. Now, Sister Amnesia. Try to remember what I teach in the novitiate:
Gentle, but firm. *(She stomps her foot.)*

SR. AMNESIA. Gentle, but firm!

*(Pause...***SR. HUBERT*** *points to* **SR. AMNESIA***'s foot and she stomps it.* **SR. HUBERT** *exits left making the sign of the cross as she goes.* **SR. AMNESIA** *takes a deep breath and snaps to attention, ruler in hand.)*

Alright! Sit up straight! Eyes forward! Pay attention! Do you know what time it is?!

(She hits the palm of her hand with the ruler. It obviously hurts and she grimaces, rubbing her hand on her thigh. She reverts to her wide-eyed innocent self.)

You know, I always know what time it is. Because back at the convent we have this huge clock with the twelve apostles pasted on it. And I always know when the big hand is on the John and the little hand is on the Peter it's time for the sisters to go down on their knees... and pray!

And now it's time for that quiz that Reverend Mother warned you about. *(She takes the index cards with the questions out of her pocket and hooks the ruler on her belt.)* Okay! Here are the questions that you should have the answers to, if you were paying attention to that last song. Could I have some lights, please? *(house lights up)* Oh, thank-you.

Now if you know the answer, raise your hand. Are you ready? *(She waits for response, which is usually weak.)* Are you ready?! *(response)* Good! Question number one: The leper colony was established on an island south of _____.

(Audience yells out "France.")

SR. AMNESIA. I asked you to raise your hands! Alright. I'm going to give you one more chanc – same question. The Leper colony was established on an island south of_____.

(She calls on someone.)

Would you have known the answer if everyone hadn't blurted it out? *(Audience member responds.)* Good, you're honest. I have a prize for you.

(She goes into the audience. If there is a balcony, she hollers: "Now you people in the balcony, don't feel left out. After all, you're closer to heaven!"*)*

(She goes to the winner, holding the prize up for all to see.) Look everybody, it's a genuine Saint Christopher Motorist Prayer Card! And see, it says here, "I am a Catholic. In case of accident, please call a priest.

(to winner) Are you Catholic?

(If, yes:)	*(If no:)*
Oh, good! Then you won't have to scratch anything out. But if you're Catholic you should know that you're supposed to stand up when Sister calls on you.	I knew that. You know why? If you were Catholic you'd know that you're supposed to stand up when Sister calls on you. What are you? *(Winner answers)* Who do you call? *(Winner answers)* Well, then you just scratch this out and write in "In case of accident please call _____").

Now I must tell you. Saint Christopher is no longer a saint. Yeah. I think he must've had an accident or something. I guess that's why we got these at a discount. So buckle up! Give our winner a hand everybody!

(**SR. AMNESIA** *returns to the stage.*)

SR. AMNESIA. Okay. Question number two. This is harder than the first one. Why?

(She pauses for a moment and then realizes there is more to the question.) Oh! Why did the sisters leave the leper colony?

[MUSIC NO. 05A: "QUIZ TIMER"]

(The timer music plays until **SR. AMNESIA** *hears the correct answer. The answer is: "They lost the race to the Protestants." But Sister usually accepts anything to do with the race/condos etc. to keep the show pace up. If no hands raise she says, "I'll give you a hint." She mimes racing and indicating her nose falls off. Whatever answer she gets she says "Close enough!")*

[MUSIC NO. 05B: "QUIZ FANFARE"]

(She goes into the audience to the next winner, making sure the winner stands up. She holds the prize up for all to see.)

It's a holy card of a saint! Do you know who he is? *(Hint: He liked animals and little birds…)* It's Saint Francis! You know some people think Saint Francis was a sissy! But that's not right! Reverend Mother explained to me that he was of Assisi. That's very different. Give our winner a hand. *(Winner sits down.)*

Okay…how many Catholics do we have here tonight! *(She picks someone.)* I have a prize for you just for being Catholic! I bet you never thought it would pay off! *(giving prize)* For you I have a medal of a saint. That's Saint Dymphna. She's the patron saint of people with mental disorders. Reverend Mother says I should pray to her everyday!

Hold mic in face & if they start to mouth off turn off mic.

(**SR. AMNESIA** *goes back to the stage.*) ↑SL stairs & OS

Now I have one last question that Sister Hubert wanted me to ask.

(REV. MOTHER sticks her head out stage left to hear what's going on.)

Do you think it was wrong for Reverend Mother to buy a Plasma TV before all of the sisters were buried?

(REV. MOTHER comes rushing on and whisks SR. AMNESIA off stage right. SR. AMNESIA protests:)

SR. AMNESIA. But they didn't answer.

[MUSIC NO. 05C: "QUIZ FANFARE"]

(REV. MOTHER returns to center stage.)

REV. MOTHER. Well, I think that's about enough time on the quiz. Now, I'd like to present Sister Mary Leo in her interpretation of "Morning at the Convent." Sister –

Iv *[MUSIC NO. 06: "BENEDICITE"]*

(REV. MOTHER exits right as SR. LEO enters left wearing a bathrobe and huge fluffy slippers which are covering her pointe shoes. She carries a Teddy Bear. She sits on the bed.)

SR. LEO.
I WAKE UP ALL BLEARY
WHEN I FIRST HEAR THE
AGE OLD QUERY:

SR. HUBERT. *(Sticking her head in stage left:)*
BENEDICITE. *(then disappears)*

SR. LEO.
DOMINUS.
THANK GOD WE CAN'T SPEAK TO EACH OTHER,
I'M NOT IN THE MOOD TO BE CHEERY.

(She stands and removes the robe. She is underdressed in her habit.)

PUT ON THE TUNIC AND SCAPULAR,
THEN THE WIMPLE – LOOK, NO MIRROR!
THE GUIMPE AND VEIL
COMPLETE THE NUN'S COUTURE.

(She sits back down on the bed.)

SR. LEO.

AT AN UNGODLY HOUR
THE BELL IN THE TOWER
SIGNALS A WARNING.

(The school bell rings loudly. If a hand bell is used **SR. HUBERT** *rings it.)*

WE'VE MADE IT THROUGH
ONE MORE NIGHT.
IT'S TIME TO GREET A NEW MORNING.

BUT BEFORE I GO DOWNSTAIRS
I CLEAR MY HEAD OF WOES AND CARES
BY DANCING MY WAY
THROUGH MY MORNING PRAYERS.

(She removes her slippers revealing the pointe shoes and the dance begins.)

DANCING IS THE WAY I PRAY.
I CAN HAVE A PERFECT DAY,
IF I START OFF WITH A TOUR JETE!

(Strip music starts and **SR. LEO** *starts belting the song.* **SR. HUBERT** *appears stage left.)*

SO IF YOU WAKE UP FEELING BLAH,
TRY MY PROVEN FORMULA.

SR. HUBERT. Sister!

*(***SR. LEO*** *sees* **SR. HUBERT** *and looks appropriately apologetic.* **SR. HUBERT** *disappears.)*

POINTE YOUR TOES AND PLIÉ.
ONCE EACH DAY!

[MUSIC NO. 06A: "BENEDICITE PLAYOFF"]

*(***SR. LEO*** *acknowledges applause.* **SR. HUBERT** *enters stage left carrying* **SR. LEO***'S street shoes.)*

SR. HUBERT. Sister Mary Leo that was just wonderful. I wish I could dance like you do!

(**SR. LEO** *takes the shoes from* **SR. HUBERT**, *goes and sits on the bed and begins changing her shoes, all the while continuing the conversation.*)

SR. LEO. Well, you could have seen a lot more but Reverend Mother won't let me wear a tutu.

SR. HUBERT. *(moving toward the bed)* Now, you know how Reverend Mother feels about the traditional habit.

SR. LEO. I know. "If God had wanted everyone to look like people…

SR. HUBERT & SR. LEO. …He wouldn't have invented nuns!"

(They both "ZZZZZZT" each other with their index fingers mocking Reverend Mother.)

SR. HUBERT. That's right.

SR. LEO. But when I entered the convent I planned to dedicate my life to God through the dance. If I can't wear a tutu, I'll never become a famous nun ballerina!

[MUSIC NO. 07: "THE BIGGEST AIN'T THE BEST"]

SR. HUBERT. Sister Mary Leo! Have you forgotten about humility?

*(**SR. LEO** looks embarrassed. **SR. HUBERT** moves downstage center and sings directly to the audience.)*

I'VE ALWAYS TAUGHT THE NOVICES
THAT GOD IS ON THEIR SIDE,
WHEN THEY'RE LOOKING FOR THE STRENGTH
TO AVOID THE SIN OF PRIDE.

SR. LEO. *(sitting on the bed; responds)*
I KNOW THAT BEING HUMBLE
IS A VIRTUE WE HOLD DEAR.
BUT HOW CAN I BE HUMBLE
AND ADVANCE IN MY CAREER?

SR. HUBERT. Sister Mary Leo! Your vocation is your career. *(to audience)* Would you excuse me for a moment? *(She goes and sits on the bed next to **SR. LEO**.)* Sister, I'd like to say something before this goes any further. You see,

I wanted to be a nun ever since I was a little girl. My dream was to enter the convent...

(She looks off to stage right where **REV. MOTHER** *exited to be sure she isn't listening.)*

SR. HUBERT. ...Work my way up to Mother Superior, and then turn the Little Sisters of Hoboken into *(She stands and with great gusto shouts:)* – the BIG SISTERS OF NEWARK! Well, the first lesson I had to learn upon entering the convent was that we do not strive for position – just perfection. Besides *(She imparts her strategy.)* she who exalts herself shall be humbled. But she who humbles herself *(again with gusto)* shall be exalted!

*(***SR. HUBERT*** sits back down on the bed and continues the song.)*

REVEREND MOTHER IS THE BOSS
AND SO I MUST OBEY.
BUT AS MISTRESS OF THE NOVICES
I SHINE IN MY OWN WAY.

SR. LEO.

YOU MEAN IF I'M REALLY HUMBLE
I COULD HAVE A SHOT
AT A BIT OF EXAULTATION
WITH MY SIMPLE LOT?

SR. HUBERT.

YOU, GOT IT, KID!
THE BIGGEST AIN'T THE BEST.
VERY OFTEN WE'RE IMPRESSED
BY A TINY DIAMOND CHIP
THAT SEEMS TO OUTSHINE ALL THE REST.

SO PAY ATTENTION NOW.
HERE'S WHAT YOU MUST DO.
DON'T DEMAND THE SPOTLIGHT.
LET THE SPOTLIGHT COME TO YOU.

(The spotlight comes on to **SR. HUBERT** *and then moves to* **SR. LEO**.*)*

SR. LEO. I'm beginning to see the light.

SR. HUBERT.

REMEMBER SISTER HILDA
WHOSE ENDOWMENT WAS SO GREAT?

SR. LEO.

WHEN SHE PUT ON HER COLLAR
IT STOOD OUT LIKE A PLATE.

*(**SR. LEO** holds her collar out straight.)*

SR. HUBERT.

WELL, ONE DAY WHEN THE BISHOP CAME
AND SHE WENT TO THE DOOR,
AS SHE KNELT TO KISS HIS RING
SHE FELL FLAT OUT ON THE FLOOR –

*(**SR. HUBERT** starts to fall forward off the bed. **SR. LEO** grabs her so she doesn't hit the floor.)*

– AND PROVED:

BOTH.

THE BIGGEST AIN'T THE BESSED,
AS THE BISHOP WILL ATTEST.
THE LORD TELL US THE LEAST
ARE OFTEN THOSE THAT ARE THE BLEST.

SR. HUBERT.

SO LET THAT BE A LESSON TO YOU.
TRY TO UNDERSTAND.
THE PEOPLE WITH THE BIGGEST DRUMS
DON'T ALWAYS LEAD THE BAND!

BOTH. *(moving down center)*

OH, THE BIGGEST AIN'T THE BEST
VERY OFTEN WE'RE IMPRESSED
BY A TINY DIAMOND CHIP
THAT SEEMS TO OUTSHINE ALL THE REST.

SR. HUBERT.

SO DO WHAT YOU DO WELL.

SR. LEO.

I KNOW I'LL BE FINE. *(She crosses herself.)*

SR. HUBERT.
> JUST REMEMBER TO BE HUMBLE.
>
> (**SR. LEO** *genuflects.*)

BOTH.
> AS WE PROUDLY GO AND –

SR. HUBERT.
> SMILE, BABY!

SR. LEO.
> SPARKLE, NEELY!

BOTH.
> SING OUT, LOUISE!
> – AND SHINE!
>
> (**REV. MOTHER** *enters stage right, applauding.*)

Iv

[MUSIC NO. 08: "ROBERT ANNE'S SURPRISE"]

> (**SR. ROBERT ANNE** *enters on upper platform and then comes down stairs to* **REV. MOTHER**. *She has her veil twisted into a turban with artificial fruit hanging from it. She is shaking a pair of maracas.*)

SR. ROBERT ANNE. Well, what dy'a think? I call it the Convent Miranda look.

> (**SR. LEO** *and* **SR. HUBERT** *realize there is going to be trouble and sneak off stage left taking the bathrobe, toe shoes and Teddy Bear with them.*)

REV. MOTHER. Sister! I am appalled! Now, you show some respect!

SR. ROBERT ANNE. C'mon…chill out, Rev. (*She puts her props on the lunch counter and fixes her veil properly.*) Listen, I've got another little surprise for you.

REV. MOTHER. Another surprise?

SR. ROBERT ANNE. (*to* **REV. MOTHER**) *See,* I realized when you arranged the program you hadn't included a solo for me and so I've been working on a special song with Father Patrick and I thought you could find a spot for it in the show. Listen to this. Hit it, Pat.

(During the above speech **REV. MOTHER** *is trying to stop* **SR. ROBERT ANNE**. *She shakes her head no, etc.)*

[MUSIC NO. 08A: "ANOTHER SURPRISE"]

WHEN I BECAME A NUN,
AT A VERY EARLY AGE.
I HAD TO CHOOSE BETWEEN THE CONVENT AND A –

REV. MOTHER. *(interrupting)* Sister…Sister!

(Music out.)

Sister Robert Anne. You are the understudy. Do you realize what a great honor and responsibility that is? You must be ready at a moment's notice in case an emergency should arise. Take me, for example. I am the Mother Superior not a musical comedy star!

[MUSIC NO. 09: "PLAYING SECOND FIDDLE"]

SR. ROBERT ANNE. *(aside to audience)* I realized that from the opening number!

REV. MOTHER. *(fuming)* Why, I oughta…

SR. ROBERT ANNE. Hey, listen:

(to **REV. MOTHER***)* I DON'T MEAN TO SOUND UNGRATEFUL,
BUT I'D RATHER HAVE A SPOT
THAT IS JUST FOR ROBERT ANNE.
I'M NOT ASKING FOR A LOT.
AN UNDERSTUDY NEVER SHINES
UNTIL THE STAR IS ILL.
THEN THE CROWD IS HOSTILE.
THE STAR'S NOT ON THE BILL!

REV. MOTHER. Sister, I don't believe this is something to discuss in front of the audience.

SR. ROBERT ANNE.

PLAYING SECOND FIDDLE
POSITIVELY MEANS THIS KID'LL
NEVER GET A MOMENT
ON THE STAGE ALONE.
EVEN, GOD FORBID,
IF SOMETHING HAPPENED
AND YOU DID GET SICK –

(A look of glee comes over SR. ROBERT ANNE's face. She crosses herself and then mimes getting sick to her stomach.)

REV. MOTHER. Yes…

SR. ROBERT ANNE.

AN UNDERSTUDIED PART
IS NOT MY OWN.

I've been reading up on being an understudy and believe me, it's not encouraging.

(She pulls a book out from under her scapular which she has tucked in her belt. It is titled "The Understudy." She opens it and hands it to REV. MOTHER.)

Here, read!

WHO HERE KNOWS THAT DOLLY LEVI'S
ALSO BIBI OSTERWALD?
CAROL CHANNING WASN'T SICK
SO BIBI WASN'T CALLED.
THIS GIRL, LENORA NEMETZ,
HAS IT ON HER RESUME
THAT SHE UNDERSTUDIED EVERYONE.
WHERE IS SHE TODAY?

REV. MOTHER. *(pointing to a page in the book)* Well, there's Shirley MacLaine.

SR. ROBERT ANNE. No, No!

SHIRLEY DOESN'T COUNT.
THAT WAS JUST BIZARRE.
CAROL HANEY BREAKS HER LEG
AND SHIRLEY IS A STAR.
BUT THAT'S ABOUT AS RARE
AS LANA TURNER DOWN AT SCHWAB'S.
IT'S A MIRACLE WHEN UNDERSTUDIES
GET THE STARRING JOBS!

REV. MOTHER. Well, then I'd start prayin' if I were you.

SR. ROBERT ANNE. For what?

REV. MOTHER. A miracle!

SR. ROBERT ANNE. Give me a break!

> PLAYING SECOND FIDDLE
> POSITIVELY MEANS THIS KID'LL
> NEVER GET A LEAD
> CAUSE EVERYBODY KNOWS
> WHOEVER UNDERSTUDIED MERMAN
> AS THE GYPSY MAMA
> PERMANENTLY ENDED UP AS
> "SECOND HAND ROSE."

SR. AMNESIA. *(yelling from offstage)* Rev. Mother – I'm ready!

REV. MOTHER. I've got to get Amnesia out here for her number. We'll talk about this later.

SR. ROBERT ANNE. Her number! You gave her a number. She can't even remember who she is. My number's ready to go. Come on, Rev. I've got aspirations.

REV. MOTHER. Well, you can kiss your aspirations good-by!

SR. ROBERT ANNE. *(with great frustration)* Oh!

> **(REV. MOTHER** *exits right, carrying the maracas, fruit, and Understudy book.* **SR. ROBERT ANNE** *comes center stage and continues the song.)*

[MUSIC NO. 09A: "SECOND FIDDLE CONCLUSION"]

> I'VE GOT TO FIGURE OUT A WAY
> TO GET A SOLO SPOT,
> SO I CAN PROVE TO REV'REND MOTHER
> WHAT IT TAKES, I GOT.
> MAYBE THEN SHE'LL UNDERSTAND
> THIS FEELING IN MY SOUL –

FR. PATRICK. *(looking offstage right)* Robert Anne, she's coming back.

SR. ROBERT ANNE.

> THAT I DESERVE A LEADING ROLE!

> **(SR. ROBERT ANNE** *starts to exit right as* **REV. MOTHER** *enters right followed by* **SRS. AMNESIA, HUBERT,** *&* **LEO. SR. HUBERT** *stops* **SR. ROBERT ANNE** *from exiting*

and they sit at the counter. **SR. LEO** *takes her place on the stool next to the juke box as* **REV. MOTHER** *comes center stage with* **SR. AMNESIA** *standing behind her. The applause from the audience for* **SR. ROBERT ANNE** *is acknowledged by* **REV. MOTHER** *as if it is for her.*)

REV. MOTHER. Oh, you don't have to applaud every time I come on. You know, I feel personally responsible for the predicament that's brought us here. You see, Sr. Julia has never been able to get a handle on her vocation. Only last week we had the Monsignor over for dinner so I asked Julia to prepare something a little special. A few minutes later I see her in the kitchen setting up the ironing board. I says, "Julia, what the hell are you doing?"

(SR. JULIA enters from the left carrying an iron.)

SR. JULIA. I said, "I'm making pressed duck!"

REV. MOTHER. Oh, good heavens! Ladies and gentlemen: Sister Julia *(all cross themselves)* Child of God. Where have you been? You missed half the show.

SR. JULIA. I was at the convent working on my new chicken recipe so we'd have something to eat after the show. I guess I got a little behind schedule.

REV. MOTHER. *(indicating the iron)* So are you pressing chicken now?

SR. JULIA. Oh, Reverend Mother, don't be silly. You don't press chicken. I was just showing the guys in the back how I could fry bacon with my iron. *(She smells the iron.)* Smells just like Sunday morning. Mmmm, mmm!
Hey, ya wanna hear something funny?

REV. MOTHER. I can't wait.

SR. JULIA. Ask me how you get down off a duck.

REV. MOTHER. How do you get down off a duck?

SR. JULIA. How'd you get up there in the first place?

(SR. JULIA laughs at her own joke. REV. MOTHER is embarrassed.)

REV. MOTHER. Ya know folks, this isn't easy. We used to have _____ *(the number of nuns appearing in the show plus 52)* members in our order, but thanks to you-know-who we're down to ____ *(the number appearing in the show)*

SR. JULIA. You know that was an accident.

REV. MOTHER. We all know that, but we're still short fifty-two sisters.

SR. JULIA. Well, maybe if people in our audience knew a little more about us, some of them would be interested...

(SR. AMNESIA is tugging on REV. MOTHER's veil.)

(irritated) What?! What is it?

SR. AMNESIA. *(in a loud whisper)* Reverend Mother, I thought I was supposed to do this part.

REV. MOTHER. Oh, dear. I'm sorry. *(to SR. JULIA)* I promised Sister here that she could do this part.

(to SR. AMNESIA) You go right ahead, dear. I forgot.

(REV. MOTHER starts exiting right with SR. JULIA.)

It must be catching. Julia, I'm sorry.

SR. JULIA. *(Holding up the iron, very indignantly.)* Talk to the iron.

[MUSIC NO. 10: "SO YOU WANT TO BE A NUN"]

(SR. JULIA sits down next to SR. HUBERT and puts the iron on the counter. As REV. MOTHER passes SR. HUBERT to exit she adds:)

Keep an eye on her *(indicating SR. AMNESIA)* Hubert.

(As the music starts, SRS. BRENDAN, LUKE, and a few members of the chorus "sneak in" at various entrances to listen.)

SR. AMNESIA. *(center stage)* Hello. My name is Sister Mary *(pause)* oh, for a minute there I thought I remembered my real name. Anyway, I'm here to tell you what being a nun means to me. Reverend Mother tells me she is certain that if I give a good talk at least one of you will want to join our order. And I think it might be you – my *(She mentions the religion of a person she picked in the quiz.)* friend! I think it is just wonderful –
– THAT YOU WANT TO BE A NUN.
AND YOU THINK IT MIGHT BE FUN
TO BE ONE OF THE ONE'S WHO'S A NUN.

(She looks to the others for approval. They nod and clap politely.)

THEN THE ORDER YOU ELECT TO SELECT
SHOULD REFLECT, I SUSPECT
A DESIRE TO PERFECT ALL YOU'VE DONE
UP TILL NOW.
I WISH THAT SOMEHOW –

*(**SR. MARY ANNETTE,** the nun puppet, suddenly appears. **SR. AMNESIA** has had her behind her back. **SR. AMNESIA** uses a crass speaking voice for **SR. MARY ANNETTE**. She is not a ventriloquist.)*

SR. MARY ANNETTE. Stop! I can't stand listening to this.

SR. AMNESIA. Sister Mary Annette! *(The puppet bows.)* What are you doing here? I thought you stayed in France with the Protestants!

SR. MARY ANNETTE. No way, Jose. *(to audience)* Girls, if you want to be a nun, join an order that still wears a habit!

SR. AMNESIA. Now, wait a minute, Sister. It's true that we still wear our habits to retain our magic spell, but even I know "a habit does not a nun make!"

SR. MARY ANNETTE. Oh, get real will ya! *(to Conductor)* Hit it, Schweetheart!
IT'S REALLY VERY SIMPLE
WITH A WIMPLE YOU'LL LEARN
YOU GET INSTANT RESPECT

WHICH YOU DON'T HAVE TO EARN.
YOU MOVE RIGHT UP IN LINES
WITHOUT WAITING YOUR TURN.
VIRTUES LIKE PATIENCE
ARE NOT OUR CONCERN!

SR. AMNESIA. Oh, now Sister. I thought virtue was always our concern.

THINK ABOUT OUR SOLEMN VOWS.
THERE ARE THREE WE MUST ESPOUSE.
POVERTY, CHASTITY, AND OBEDIENCE,
(very loudly) NOW –

SR. MARY ANNETTE. What the hell are you trying to do? Make me go deaf?

SR. MARY AMNESIA. Don't be silly, Sister. You can't go deaf. Everyone can see, "Nuns don't have ears!" Now where was I?

(The puppet whispers something to **SR. AMNESIA.***)*

Oh, yeah.

LET'S START WITH POVERTY EMPTY YOUR PURSE.
POVERTY MAKES BEING POOR EVEN WORSE!
GRANTED, IT'S NOT SO EXTREME FOR A NUN.
WE MAY NOT BE STARVING, BUT STILL IT'S NOT FUN.

NOT FUN, NOT FUN, NOT FUN, NOT FUN, NOT FUN!
NOT FUN, NOT FUN, NOT FUN, NOT FUN, NOT FUN!
NOT FUN, NOT FUN, NOT FUN, NOT FUN, NOT F-U-N!
POVERTY'S NOT FUN.

SR. MARY ANNETTE. What d'ya mean, poverty's not fun?

YOU CAN'T DENY WE LIVE LIKE WE'RE FROM BEVERLY HILLS
WHILE MOTHER SUPERIOR PAYS ALL THE BILLS.
WAKE UP! SMELL THE COFFEE, GIRL! OUR LIVES
ARE FIRST-RATE.
FROM A NUN'S POINT OF VIEW, POVERTY'S GREAT!

SR. AMNESIA. What are you talking about, "poverty's great?"

SR. MARY ANNETTE. Well, isn't it obvious? We can have everything. We just can't own it!

SR. AMNESIA. *(looking embarrassed)* Oh…
>CHASTITY IS WHERE WE'VE FOUND
>OUR POSTULANTS ARE LOSING GROUND.
>YOU MUST BE CELIBATE.

SR. MARY ANNETTE.
>YOU CAN'T SCREW AROUND!

SR. AMNESIA. *(shocked)*
>SISTER!
>OBEDIENCE IN NUMBER THREE.
>WE CANNOT QUESTION WHAT WILL BE.
>IF YOU HAVE NO OPINIONS
>THE LIVIN' IS EASY –

Wait a minute. I think I'm beginning to remember who I am.

SR. MARY ANNETTE. Yeah. And the fish are jumpin' and the cotton is high. Can get we get back to obedience?
>IF PAIN CAN MAKE YOU PERFECT
>THEN THIS VOW IS FOR YOU.
>EVERYTIME YOU DISOBEY
>THEY BEAT YOUR ASS BLACK AND BLUE!

SR. AMNESIA. *(mortified)*
>THE CONFESSIONAL'S WHERE SHE BELONGS.
>EVERYTHING SHE SAYS IS WRONG.

SR. MARY ANNETTE.
>SISTER'S JUST JEALOUS CAUSE I STOLE HER SONG.

SR. AMNESIA.
>DEDICATION AND COMMITMENT –

SR. MARY ANNETTE.
>YOU'RE SO FULL OF –

SR. AMNESIA.
>DON'T FINISH THAT ONE!

SR. MARY ANNETTE.
>NO HABIT, NO TICKET TO FUN!

SR. AMNESIA. *(pointing her finger at* **SR. MARY ANNETTE***)*
>THIS SONG IS –

>*(***SR. MARY ANNETTE*** bites* **SR. AMNESIA***'s finger.)*

>OOOOWWW –

SR. MARY ANNETTE. Get the hook!

SR. AMNESIA. DONE!

[MUSIC NO. 10A: "NUN PLAYOFF"] confused applause

(REV. MOTHER enters right, sees SR. AMNESIA and chases her and the puppet off left. All of the chorus people exit, knowing there will be trouble.)

I vii **REV. MOTHER.** Why didn't someone tell me she brought I vii that puppet?

SR. ROBERT ANNE. Don't look at me!

SRS. LEO, LUKE & BRENDAN. Who knew?

REV. MOTHER. *(to SR. HUBERT)* You knew! I know you knew!

SR. HUBERT. *(SR. HUBERT starts laughing.)* Well, I knew about the puppet, but I had no idea she was gonna –

REV. MOTHER. *(interrupting)* What if we have some plain-clothes nuns in our audience? I certainly hope no one was offended.

SR. HUBERT. Please don't let this affect your generosity this evening.

REV. MOTHER. Really! We've just gotta get those girls out of the freezer!

I mean, you never know when the Health Inspector might be coming around.

SR. AMNESIA. *(re-entering from left totally innocently, without the puppet)* Did I miss something?

REV. MOTHER. Just the boat, dear.

SR. AMNESIA. Oh, Reverend Mother. We don't have a boat. Sister *(indicating SR. ROBERT ANNE)* drove the car!

SR. LEO. *(getting up from the stool)* Amnesia, Reverend Mother was just saying that she didn't know when the Health Inspector might be coming around.

SR. AMNESIA. Oh, he's coming this week.

REV. MOTHER. What do you mean, "he's coming this week?"

SR. AMNESIA. He called yesterday.

ALL BUT SR. AMNESIA. What?!

(SR. ROBERT ANNE *jumps up from the bar stool.*)

REV. MOTHER. Amnesia, why don't you tell me these things?

SR. AMNESIA & REV. MOTHER. *(in unison)* I forgot.

REV. MOTHER. Oh, this is terrible. Amnesia, go and phone the convent right away and see if anything's happened.

go
to JUDY
(platform)

(SR. AMNESIA *runs up the steps to the phone while* SRS. ROBERT ANNE, LEO, LUKE & BRENDAN *gather around the jukebox. Simultaneously* REV. MOTHER *goes over to* SR. HUBERT *at the counter.*)

(REV. MOTHER *continues.*) This is just awful. Lord only knows what may have happened. Sister Hubert, I thought I told you to see that she reports everything to me!

SR. HUBERT. Now, don't you try to blame this one on me. You're the one who bought the Plasma TV!

REV. MOTHER. Don't start with that. You know very well I didn't realize there wasn't enough money.

[MUSIC NO. 11: "MOCK FIFTIES"]

(SR. ROBERT ANNE *accidentally starts the juke box and the four Sisters start 50s-style dancing.* REV. MOTHER *runs over to stop things and* SR. ROBERT ANNE *grabs her and pulls her into the dance.*)

SRS. LEO, ROBERT ANNE, LUKE & BRENDAN.
SHA NA NA NA NA NA,
SHA NA NA NA NA NA,
SHA NA NA NA NA NA, NA! NA!

REV. MOTHER. Stop it! Stop it! Turn that thing off!

(FR. VIRGIL *and* SR. WILHELM *enter left hurriedly.*)

SR. WILHELM. We got here as soon as we could.

FR. VIRGIL. We've got news.

REV. MOTHER. Ladies and gentlemen, Sister Mary Wilhelm, our nurse. And Father Virgil, our Chaplain.
What's this about news? I thought you were at the convent.

FR. VIRGIL. We were, but then Sister Marie Eugene got a call from the health department and we figured you'd want to know.

SR. WILHELM. They told her they were on their way over for an inspection.

SR. LUKE. *(If the show is in the afternoon:)* Uh-oh!
(If the show is in the evening:) At this hour? Boy they are sneaky.

SR. BRENDAN. What are you going to do?

REV. MOTHER. *(going over to* **SR. HUBERT***)* Hubert...

SR. HUBERT. Don't look at me. I'm only number two... remember?

FR. VIRGIL. There's not much you can do right now. Besides, the reason you're here on the stage is to fix the problem.

SR. LUKE. Father's right.

[MUSIC NO. 11A: "A GOOD CAUSE"]

SR. BRENDAN.

IT'S FOR A GOOD CAUSE
THAT WE'RE PUTTIN' ON THIS SHOW.

SR. WILHELM.

WE'VE GOTTA GET THOSE GIRLS IN THE GROUND.

ALL SEVEN.

IT'S FOR A GOOD CAUSE,

FR. VIRGIL.

HEY, YOU JUST NEVER KNOW
WHEN THE HEALTH INSPECTOR MIGHT COME AROUND.

SR. WILHELM.

AND IT'S FAIR TO SUPPOSE
IF HE STICKS HIS NOSE
INSIDE OUR CONVENT FRIDGE,

SR. JULIA.

HE AIN'T GONNA LEAVE
THINKING HE'S SEEN A FOURSOME
HANGIN' THERE PLAYIN' BRIDGE.

No Stomps!

ALL SEVEN.

> WE KNOW WE'LL REACH OUR GOAL
> TO PLANT THE FOUR IN CLOVER
> IF EACH OF YOU GIVES A FAIR SHARE.
> SO WON'T-CHA DIG DOWN DEEP
> SO WE CAN GET THIS OVER.
> SHOW THE ALMIGHTY YOU CARE.
> IT'S FOR A GREAT CAUSE,

Clasp hands on ♥

SRS. JULIA & WILHELM.

> YOU REALLY CAN'T DENY IT,
> AFTER ALL IS SAID AND DONE.

ALL SEVEN.

> IT'S FOR A GREAT CAUSE

FR. VIRGIL.

> THE LORD WOULD SANCTIFY IT.

ALL SEVEN.

> WHO CAN REFUSE A DEAD NUN?
>
> SO WHEN WE PASS THE PLATE
> WE'LL BE GRATEFUL
> FOR ANYTHING YOU CAN DO.

to #16

SR. JULIA.

> PLEASE BE GENEROUS TO A FAULT.

ALL SEVEN.

> OUR ONE LAST HOPE IS

FR. VIRGIL.

> YOU!

ALL SEVEN.

> BECAUSE IT'S A GOOD CAUSE
> IT'S A
> G-O-O-D
> GOOD, GOOD CAUSE!

STEP ON HIPS

> *(Music out.* **SR. AMNESIA** *comes running toward* **REV. MOTHER** *after hanging up the phone.)*

I viii

SR. AMNESIA. Reverend Mother. Reverend Mother, I kept calling and calling and it just kept ringing and ringing but finally I got the answering machine.

REV. MOTHER. Well, what did it say?

SR. AMNESIA. *(in her most sophisticated voice)* Hello. You have reached the Convent of Mount Saint Helen's –

REV. MOTHER. *(interrupting)* Amnesia! Jump ahead!

SR. AMNESIA. *(Looks at* **REV. MOTHER** *for a moment, takes a deep breath and, like a tape recorder running at "Minnie Mouse" speed, starts:)* Hello, you have reached the Convent of Mount Saint Helen's…*(gibberish…ending with)* beeeeeeeeeeeeep! *(pause)* and Sister Marie Eugene had to go down to the Board of Health for questioning!

(Everyone looks horrified.)

REV. MOTHER. Oh, no! Now you've done it, Amnesia. You should have told me they called yesterday. Now you've really done it! This is a fine mess you've gotten us into!

SR. AMNESIA. *(starts to cry)* But, I didn't mean to. I'm sorry. I didn't mean to!

awkward!

(SR. AMNESIA runs out left followed by **SRS. ROBERT ANNE, LEO, BRENDAN, LUKE, WILHELM, JULIA** *&* **FR. VIRGIL,** *all trying to calm her.* **SR. HUBERT** *gets up from the counter and comes to* **REV. MOTHER.**)

sneak out

SR. HUBERT. Regina, you didn't have to be so hard on her.

REV. MOTHER. Oh, you know I didn't mean it. Go and see if she's alright.

SR. HUBERT. Me!?

REV. MOTHER. Yes, you!

SR. HUBERT. *(starting toward left door)* Tote that barge. Lift that bale. What is this? Showboat! *(She exits.)*

Tviii

REV. MOTHER. I tell ya, it's not easy being a Mother Superior these days. Trying to be a leader in these permissive times is almost impossible. Take Sister Robert Anne for example. When she entered the convent they told me she was streetwise. Now, I thought that meant she knew her way around town! That girl knows things you couldn't show on Cable television. Why, just this morning she comes into my office and says she's writing a book for her gym class on feminine hygiene.

Do you know what she's gonna call it? The Catholic Girl's Guide to an Immaculate Conception! I'm tellin' you, it is not easy!

Sometimes I wonder why I ever became a nun in the first place. I didn't have to, ya know. *(She flicks her veil off her shoulders like a movie star pushing her long hair back.)* I started out as a tightrope walker! – I'm not makin' this up! My mother and father had a high wire act. They were billed as "Two Tons on a Tightrope!" Well, our whole family's a bit on the hefty side. My father said if we worked real hard we could be better than the Flying Wallendas – all us kids were in the act – well, all except Mary Claire – that's our sister. She took up with a contortionist and one night they were trying out a new position when, uh, well, uh *(She realizes her story is getting embarrassing.)* – that's another story. I was telling you about the act. Anyway, we got booked in London and we had a wire stretched across the river – no net mind you! Well, "Two Tons on a Tightrope" were up there when suddenly the wire snapped and BOOM – BOOM – Two Tons in the Thames! Right then and there I promised the Lord if He'd save them I'd become a nun! Well, how did I know He was gonna come through?! I thought they were gonners for sure! Well, since the Lord kept His part of the bargain, I figured I'd better keep mine, so here I am. But you wanna know the truth? *(very touchingly)* Now that I'm here, I wouldn't have it any other way.

Still, I gotta tell ya something.

[MUSIC NO. 12: TURN UP THE SPOTLIGHT]

REV. MOTHER.
I SEE THE SPOTLIGHT
AND THOUGH IT'S NOT RIGHT
I SIMPLY CAN'T RESIST IT'S CALL.
FOR SOME NUNS IT'S BINGO
AT THE PARISH HALL.
TURN UP THE SPOTLIGHT

AND I HAVE A BALL!

I LOSE MY HEAD, THEN
I KNOW I'M DEAD WHEN
I START TO HEAR THAT LAUGHTER GROW.
IT REALLY WASN'T ALL THAT LONG AGO
WHEN I WAS UP THERE
IN THE SPOTLIGHT'S GLOW.

I CAN HEAR THE BRASS BAND.
I CAN HEAR THE CROWD CHEER.
THE GRAND MARCH BEGINS.
THE CIRCUS IS HERE.

I CAN STILL HEAR THE RINGMASTER
SHOUTIN' HE'S PROUD
TO PRESENT US ON THAT WIRE
HIGH ABOVE THE CROWD!

OH, IT WAS THRILLING.
WE HAD TOP BILLING.
EVERY NIGHT WE'D STEAL THE SHOW.
PLEASE, FORGIVE ME,
BUT DON'TCHA KNOW
THIS IS MUCH MORE FUN
THAN B-I-N-G-O...OH! OH!

(REV. MOTHER has moved upstage. BR. TIMOTHY enters and hands her an umbrella. Remembering how she used the umbrella to balance herself on the tightrope, she takes it.)

I love this part! Ladies and gentlemen, how about a hand for my assistant, our stagehand, Brother Timothy! Watch this, Tim.

(She goes across the imaginary tightrope.)

TURN UP THAT SPOTLIGHT
CAUSE WHEN I'VE GOT LIGHT
I'M A BARREL FULL OF FUN.

(coming down to center stage)

REV. MOTHER.

I'M YOUR RIGHT REVEREND MAMA
SAY, "HELLO, DALAI LAMA!"
Did ya get it? "Hello, Dolly" – "Dalai Lama?"
(If audience laughs:) Oh, bless you all. Take me home, band!
(If audience groans:) Oy, vey! Take me home, band!
I'M YOUR RIGHT REVEREND MOTHER
THERE ISN'T ANY OTHER.
YOUR RIGHT REVEREND MOTHER,
SUPERIOR NUN! OH, YEAH!

[MUSIC NO. 12A: SPOTLIGHT PLAYOFF]

*(**REV. MOTHER** is doing a "strut" across the stage as **BR. TIMOTHY** applauds her and then moves the counter center stage. He is followed by **SRS. HUBERT, JULIA,** and **AMNESIA** who enter right. **BR. TIMOTHY** takes the umbrella from **REV. MOTHER** and exits left. Music out.)*

SR. JULIA. Well, you're turning out to be a regular Sophie Tucker!

*(**REV. MOTHER** looks embarrassed. **SR. AMNESIA** sits at the counter.)*

SR. AMNESIA. Was she a Mother Superior, too?

SR. HUBERT. Not quite, dear.

*(**SR. LEO** enters left, on the upper level carrying a bouquet of lilacs. She is followed by **SRS. BRENDAN** and **LUKE.** She proceeds down the steps to the stage. At first, only **SR. AMNESIA** sees her.)*

SR. AMNESIA. Lilacs.

SR. JULIA. What?

SR. AMNESIA. Li-lacs!

SR. HUBERT. *(thinking **SR. AMNESIA** is seeing things, tries to humor her)* Alright…

REV. MOTHER. *(now seeing **SR. LEO**)* Lilacs!

(**SR. AMNESIA** *mimes to the audience "I just said that –
twice!")*

*[MUSIC NO. 13: LILACS BRING BACK
MEMORIES]*

SR. HUBERT. How beautiful. Where'd they come from?

SR. LEO. There's a card. *(She hands the card to* **REV. MOTHER***.)*

REV. MOTHER. Why, they're from the ladies of the Hadassah
at Temple Beth Myerson wishing us good luck.

SR. JULIA. Wasn't that sweet of them?

SR. LEO. These sure bring back memories.

> EVERY TIME I SMELL LILACS
> I REMEMBER MY FIRST ROMANCE.

*(***REV. MOTHER** *looks shocked.)*

> I WAS PUTTING ON A BALLET IN MY BACKYARD
> WHEN I FELL IN LOVE WITH THE DANCE.

*(***REV. MOTHER** *is relieved.)*

SR. HUBERT.

> EVERY TIME I SMELL LILACS
> I REMEMBER THAT VERY SPECIAL DAY
> WHEN THE BISHOP CAME
> AND GAVE ME MY NEW NAME:
> *(looking at her ring)* Hubert – I thought I was gonna die!

SR. LEO. *(very excitedly)* Wait a minute! Wait a minute!
Amnesia, I've got an idea.

*(***FR. VIRGIL, BR. TIMOTHY** *and* **SR.WILHELM** *come on
stage from various locations thinking* **SR. AMNESIA** *will
remember her name.)*

> IF LILACS MAKE US REMEMBER THINGS
> THAT HAPPENED LONG AGO,

ALL BUT SR. AMNESIA.

> MAYBE THE FRAGRANCE CAN TAKE YOU BACKWARDS
> IN TIME TO A PLACE YOU KNOW.

*(***SR. LEO** *hands the flowers to* **SR. AMNESIA** *who buries
her head in them taking a loud audible sniff.)*

SR. AMNESIA.

> THEY SMELL VERY NICE, IT'S TRUE.
> BUT THEY DON'T REMIND ME OF ANYTHING.
> WAIT A MINUTE – YES, THEY DO!

ALL BUT SR. AMNESIA.

> THEY DO?!

SR. AMNESIA.

> I'M RUNNING THROUGH THE FIELD
> WITH THE NEIGHBOR KIDS
> WHEN I HEAR MAMA CALLING ME TO GO.
> DINNER IS READY, HURRY HOME NOW –
> BUT I CAN'T REMEMBER WHO.

ALL BUT SR. AMNESIA. *(with great disappointment)* Oh…

[MUSIC NO. 14: THE WITCH]

(There is an immediate musical segue from "Lilacs" to "The Witch." SR. ROBERT ANNE enters left "riding on a broom." She has put a funnel on her head, under her veil, creating a witch's hat.)

SR. ROBERT ANNE. *(lets out a blood-curdling screech)* I'll get you my pretty. And your little dog, too! Deedle-y-dee-dee-dee-dee. Deedle-y-dee-dee-dee-dee!

REV. MOTHER. Robert Anne! Stop that this instant! This is not "The Wizard of Oz." Who do you think you are? Margaret Hamilton?

(SR. ROBERT ANNE "ZZZZZT's" REV. MOTHER.)

Listen, Missy!

SR. ROBERT ANNE. Wait a minute! I have to tell you something important!

REV. MOTHER. Well, what is it?

SR. ROBERT ANNE. When I was in the Girls' Locker Room fixing my veil, I found this!

(SR. ROBERT ANNE pulls out a small bag from under her scapular and hands it to REV. MOTHER.)

I think one of our students has a serious problem.

FR. VIRGIL. What kind of "serious" problem?

SR. ROBERT ANNE. Look, I know about these things and I need to explain...

REV. MOTHER. *(interrupting)* You can explain it later. Right now we've got to get ready for the first act finale.

(Everyone starts asking "What's in the bag," "Let's see," etc.)

(shouting over the confusion) Hubert, get them ready for the first act finale!

SR. JULIA. I've got to go back to the convent. My chicken is probably burning!

REV. MOTHER. Fine. Go! All of you, just go!

*(**ALL** but **REV. MOTHER** and **SR. ROBERT ANNE** exit right.)*

SR. ROBERT ANNE. But, Rev...

REV. MOTHER. And get that thing out of your veil!

*(**SR. ROBERT ANNE** turns on her heels very indignantly and starts to exit right. As she gets to the bed she starts "sinking" and we hear:)*

SR. ROBERT ANNE. I'm melting...melting...melting... *(Fading, she exits.)*

REV. MOTHER. If only she could. *(Sitting down at the counter with the bag.)* I'm terribly sorry for this delay, folks. They'll only be a moment. Now what is this she's fussing about?

*(The spotlight fades up on **REV. MOTHER** as she discovers a small bottle in the bag.)*

Well, it's called "Rush." It must be something for people in a hurry. *(examining the bottle)* I guess you take a spoonful after every meal – let's see – no – it says here: "Remove cap, allow to stand, aroma will develop." Aroma? What kind of aroma?

(She opens bottle and takes a whiff.)

Ooooh – Good Lord, it smells awful! Why would anyone want this stuff? *(looking at the bottle)* R-U...R-U...*(singing)* ARE YOU LONESOME TONIGHT? Is it warm in here? I'm awfully warm. It must be the wimple. Oh, I hope I don't get wimple itch. I don't know what the girls are doing with this stuff. It can't be good for you. It smells just awful.

(She turns her back to the audience, takes a quick sniff, and then turns back. She is starting to get the giggles.)

REV. MOTHER. Is it hot in here? Whoa, it must be the lights. Alright. In a few minniments – monoments – mominna – *(laughing)* SOON –

(laughing more with a snort) We'll get back to Nundance No!

Flashnun! *(flipping the scapular in the air and laughing)* Butch Cassidy and the Sundance Nun – no, no, no. That's not right. Nun with the Wind! *(She gives a "Bronx cheer" sounding like passing gas.)* Oh, no! *(turning to the band)* What show is this?

FATHER PATRICK. *(Conductor)* Are you alright?

REV. MOTHER. *(getting up and walking toward the band)* Alright?! I've never felt better in my life. Hey, have you guys tried this stuff? Oh, of course, you have. You're musicians! *(coming back to the audience)* Have you tried this? Have you… *(picking someone in the front of the audience)* …oh, you have. I know you have.

You know this stuff is absolutely marvelous. I'm gonna take some back to the convent. *(taking a huge audible sniff)* Whoooooaaaaa! I'm going to Disney World!

*(**REV. MOTHER** goes back to sit down and regain her composure.)*

Okay. Let's all sit back and watch a coupl'a butch nuns dance. *(laughing raucously and then realizing what was said)* Did I say that? *(with right arm outstretched she hits the top of the counter three times while saying)* That's not right. *(hit three more times)* That's not right. *(looking left)* Come in! *(More laughing then turning toward center stool, she takes it like a steering wheel. In a low pitched voice:)* I got to drive Miss Daisy down to the Piggly Wiggly!

(Turning back on the stool REV. MOTHER *slips off and down to the counter floor while her habit goes over the stool making her look pregnant.)*

It's a miracle! Somebody call a donkey and get me to the manger. *(She starts to get up.)* Oh-oh. I'm stuck. I'm not kidding. I'm really stuck! Well, don't anybody come out here to help me. Never mind, I'll do it myself. *(Struggling, she gets her leg over the stool and is on the floor.)* Free Willy! Free Willy! You know, it's hot in here!

*(***SR. HUBERT*** *followed by* **SRS. LEO, AMNESIA** *and* **WILHELM** *enter right while* **SRS. BRENDAN** *and* **LUKE** *enter left.)*

SR. HUBERT. Reverend Mother!

REV. MOTHER. Hubert! I've fallen and I can't get up.

*(***SR. HUBERT*** *has changed to black tap shoes, but doesn't call attention to this fact. She and* **SR. WILHELM** *get* **REV. MOTHER** *on her feet.)*

SR. HUBERT. Turn off that –

[MUSIC NO. 15: TURN OFF THAT SPOTLIGHT]

Spotlight! *(spotlight out)*

REV. MOTHER.

WAIT! I'M NOT QUITE –

SR. WILHELM.

YES, YOU ARE.

*(***SR. HUBERT*** *&* **SR. WILHELM** *take* **REV. MOTHER** *off left as* **SRS. LEO** *and* **AMNESIA** *put the counter back.)*

SR. BRENDAN.

SHE'S STONED!

SR. LUKE.

COULD YA DIE?

*(***SR. ROBERT ANNE*** *followed by* **FR. VIRGIL** *enter left door.)*

SR. ROBERT ANNE.

WHAT'S GOING ON?

SR. LEO.

REVEREND MOTHER GOT HIGH.

SR. ROBERT ANNE.

I COULDA TOLD HER THAT STUFF MAKES YA FLY!

FR. VIRGIL.

YOU'RE GONNA FRY!

SR. ROBERT ANNE. HEY, NOW I – didn't tell her to use it!

(All start talking at once: "You're gonna get it," "You should have known better," etc. SR. HUBERT carrying a shopping bag enters right as SR. WILHELM enters left.)

SR. HUBERT.

PUT ON THESE SHOES! C'MON ALL OF YOU.
THERE'S BEEN A SLIGHT CHANGE
IN WHAT'S ABOUT TO ENSUE.

SR. ROBERT ANNE.

I THOUGHT WE PLANNED THIS SONG FOR ACT TWO.

SR. HUBERT.

WELL, WE DID. BUT IT'S NOT. WE'VE GOTTA DO IT. NOW!

(We hear raucous laughter from REV. MOTHER offstage. SR. ROBERT ANNE takes the bag and all but SR. HUBERT exit right to change to tap shoes backstage.)

[MUSIC NO. 16: TACKLE THAT TEMPTATION]

IF EVER YOU ARE TEMPTED TO TRANSGRESS, REMEMBER
    THIS:

(REV. MOTHER appears at the right:)

REV. MOTHER. Hubert! I just saw Elvis. He's alive! He's alive!

(SR. HUBERT looks as if she can't believe what's happening as REV. MOTHER disappears offstage.)

SR. HUBERT.

AN IDLE MIND IS WHERE THE DEVIL WORKS,
SO IN MY ANALYSIS –
IF BUSY HANDS ARE HAPPY HANDS
THEN DANCING FEET ARE BLISS! SO:

Real performance style of Chorus Line & Fosse

Tempo 5% faster

TACKLE THAT TEMPTATION WITH A TIME-STEP.
NOT A ONE-STEP OR A TWO-STEP, BUT A TIME-STEP.

(SR. HUBERT starts to tap dance.)

STAMP-HOP-SHUFFLE-STEP-FA-LAP-BALL-CHANGE
IN YOUR TAP SHOES.
YOU CAN CHASE THE DEVIL OUT
AND SHOUT THE GOOD NEWS.
TACKLE THAT TEMPTATION WITH A TIME-STEP
BEFORE TEMPTATION TACKLES YOU!
I SAID:

*(The entire cast with the exception of REV. MOTHER
and SR. JULIA enters from various spots singing and
dancing. All are wearing multi-colored tap shoes.)*

Don't rush

stay light tops
#12

ALL.

TACKLE THAT TEMPTATION WITH A TIME-STEP.
NOT A ONE-STEP OR A TWO-STEP, BUT A TIME-STEP.
AND IF THAT'S NOT ENOUGH, THEN GO
AND SHUFFLE OFF TO BUFFALO.
TACKLE THAT TEMPTATION WITH A TIME-STEP
BEFORE TEMPTATION TACKLES YOU!

*(Dance break occurs here featuring a tap challenge. It
can be done with four or five principals or by chorus
people or a combination of the best tappers. As ALL go
into the final section REV. MOTHER enters on the upper
level wearing the fruit hat used by SR. ROBERT ANNE
as Carmen Miranda and shaking the maracas. She
proceeds to try to join the dance.)*

pyramid
#6

chorus line #10

kick line #12

SR. HUBERT. *(seeing REV. MOTHER)* Reverend Mother!
(to others) Get her outta here. She's ruining my big
number!

(The others push her back out of the way.)

ALL BUT REV. MOTHER.

TURN UP THE SPOTLIGHT,
THOUGH THIS IS NOT QUITE
WHAT WE EXPECTED WE WOULD DO.

(REV. MOTHER breaks through the line again and is pushed back while belting out: "Gotta dance!")

ALL BUT REV. MOTHER.
WE'RE GONNA TAKE A BREAK,
PLEASE COME BACK FOR HEAVEN'S SAKE.
THERE'S A LOT MORE IN ACT TWO!

REV. MOTHER. *(sticking her head out between two Sisters)* Peek-a-boo!

ALL BUT REV. MOTHER.
UNTIL THEN –

SR. HUBERT. Get her, Robert!

(SR. ROBERT ANNE grabs REV. MOTHER as ALL head to various exits.)

REV. MOTHER. Toodle-oo!

(Blackout!)

ACT TWO

II.i

(Towards the end of intermission, **SR. HUBERT** *and several* **CHORUS MEMBERS** *go out and mingle with the audience on the orchestra floor. Some go to the balcony if there is one, otherwise they join the others. After a few minutes in the house we hear:)*

listen for
Sarah

CHORUS MEMBER #1. *(hollering over the edge of the balcony)* Sister Hubert? May I tell a joke?

SR. HUBERT. Well, I guess that would be alright.

CHORUS MEMBER #1. How do you make holy water?

SR. HUBERT. I don't know. How do you make holy water?

CHORUS MEMBER #1. You boil the hell out of it!

CHORUS MEMBER #2. I have a joke.

What did Jesus say at the Last Supper?

SR. HUBERT. What did Jesus say at the Last Supper?

CHORUS MEMBER #2. Anyone who wants to be in the picture, get on this side of the table!

CHORUS MEMBER #3. Sister Hubert, you tell your joke.

SR. HUBERT. Oh, alright. Why did Moses wander around the desert for forty years?

CHORUS MEMBER #3. Why did Moses wander around the desert for forty years?

SR. HUBERT. He was a man. And men never stop to ask for directions!

*(**SR. ROBERT ANNE** and **FR. VIRGIL** enter left door and come downstage center.)*

FR. VIRGIL. Sister Hubert, are you out there?

SR. HUBERT. Yes, what is it, Father?

FR. VIRGIL. Can you come up here? I need to talk to you.

(SR. HUBERT followed by the CHORUS MEMBERS come up on stage. The house lights fade out.)

You can go on talking, folks. We'll be starting in just a minute.

(They huddle for a moment.)

(to audience) I've just been told by Sister Wilhelm that Reverend Mother is still recovering in the Girls' Locker Room and saying an Act of Contrition. So – *(indicating* **SR. ROBERT ANNE***)* – the understudy is on! *(to the other Sisters)* C'mon, we'll get ready for the next number while Robert Anne handles everything out here.

exit

*(All but **SR. ROBERT ANNE** exit left.)*

SR. ROBERT ANNE. Alriiiiiight! Now that I have you alone for a few minutes I'd like to share something with you that I think you'll get a kick out of. And that's some more of my habit-humor. *(She pulls the sides of her veil over her shoulders and starts twisting each side, creating "braids.")* Now, you're probably wondering what nuns do in their spare time. Well, this particular nun likes to create other nuns.

*(Director's Note: If there are young kids in the cast, **SR. ROBERT ANNE** can bring them out on stage to sit in a circle around her and "guess" the names of the people she is imitating. She would say something like: Oh, you know the kids always love when I do these impressions. Come on out here kids. Let's have a round of applause for our Mt. Saint Helen's students. At the end on the impressions she would thank them and send them off before she starts "Growing Up Catholic.")*

For instance: "Toto I don't think we're in Kansas anymore. " – Sister Dorothy.

(swagging the braids) Ri – co – la! Sister Heidi.

Here's one of my favorites: *(twisting the braids around her ears)*

Help me, Obi Wan Kenobi – you are my only hope…
Oh, I got one…hang on a sec.

(She turns upstage and flipping one side of the veil up over her eye to create a white patch, she turns downstage and limps toward the audience as the band plays the "Phantom of the Opera" organ music.) If a big audience reaction: Oh, you got tickets! *If no reaction:* Nobody got tickets?

Okay, I got one more. This takes a little time so bear with me. *(to Conductor)* Hey, Father. How 'bout a little mood music?

[MUSIC NO. 17: THE VEIL]

(The following section is spoken while creating a turban.)

SR. ROBERT ANNE. You know, I do these for my students. They think they're hysterical. Of course, they love to laugh. That's how I get through to them. You know, by being funny. I teach seventh grade. That is a rough age to be. I oughta know. When I was in seventh grade I got sent to Saint Clare's School for the Deplorable. Okay, here we go. The final impression of the evening: *(à la Katherine Hepburn)* "The Callalilies are in bloom!"
(She bows and puts her veil back as it should be. Music out.)
Let's not mention this to You-Know-Who. Reverend Mother does not always appreciate my methods or my behavior. But ya gotta understand. I grew up in Canarsie. You know where that is? Brooklyn! Yo Mamma! Scungili! *(pronounced skoon-JEE-lee)* You had to be tough. And I was. I was one tough kid.

(She gets the stool from beside the juke box and brings it down center and sits.)

See, my dad was never around much and my mom had to work two jobs, so us kids were alone a lot. I was always in trouble – that's why I got sent to St. Clare's. But, hey, it's okay. Things have worked out. My background even paid off a little bit. Not only do I drive the convent car, I can strip it faster than any mechanic in Hoboken! You know a lot of the guys back in the hood still can't believe I'm a nun. But I have to tell you why. It's all because of Sister Rose Francis.

[MUSIC NO. 18: GROWING UP CATHOLIC]

SR. ROBERT ANNE. She was the Head of Saint Clare's. Boy, oh boy, she was somethin' else. She was the one person who made me believe I was worth something. And I want to be just like her. Sometimes I miss Saint Clare's. Things were really different back then. It was a long time ago.

AT SAINT CLARE'S SCHOOL, RELIGION CLASS
BEGAN WITH MASS EACH DAY.
IT WAS SAID IN LATIN THEN.
THAT'S HOW I LEARNED TO PRAY.

THE NUNS APPEARED IN BLACK AND WHITE.

(A selected number of **CHORUS NUNS** *enter upper platform and position themselves like a choir on the stairs. They "ooh" as* **SR. ROBERT ANNE** *continues singing.)*

AND SO DID EVERY RULE.
THINGS WERE EITHER WRONG OR RIGHT
AT SAINT CLARE'S CATHOLIC SCHOOL.

CHORUS NUNS.

HOSANNA!

CHORUS NUNS & SR. ROBERT ANNE.

HOSANNA!
HOSANNA IN EXCELSIS.
EXCELSIS, IN EXCELSIS.

SR. ROBERT ANNE.

BUT THEN THE RULES BEGAN TO CHANGE
AND MANY LOST THEIR WAY.
WHAT WAS ALWAYS BLACK AND WHITE
WAS TURNING SHADES OF GRAY.

CHORUS NUNS & SR. ROBERT ANNE.

HOLY, HOLY, HOLY,
HOLY LORD.

SR. ROBERT ANNE.

THOUGH MASS IS SAID IN ENGLISH NOW,
TO MAKE US MORE AWARE,
CONFUSION SEEMS TO REIGN SUPREME.
LIKE GOD, IT'S EVERYWHERE.

(The **CHORUS NUNS** *again sings "oohs.")*

THE CHURCH IS QUITE PROGRESSIVE NOW
THOUGH PEOPLE RIDICULE
THE FACT THAT SO MANY THINGS ARE OPTIONAL,
IT'S HARD TO FIND A RULE.

THROUGH IT ALL I'VE OFTEN SAID
THOSE ANCIENT LATIN PRAYERS
THAT I FIRST LEARNED WHEN GROWING UP –
CATHOLIC – AT SAINT CLARE'S.

CHORUS NUNS.

HOSANNA!

CHORUS NUNS & SR. ROBERT ANNE.

HOSANNA!
HOSANNA IN EXCELSIS!
IN EXCELSIS, IN EXCELSIS,
IN EXCELSIS!

(Lights fade out, then back up quickly. **FR. VIRGIL** *and* **BR. TIMOTHY** *enter left.* **FR. VIRGIL** *is applauding* **SR. ROBERT ANNE.** **BR. TIMOTHY** *takes the stool and puts it back in it's spot. The* **CHORUS NUNS** *come down center to congratulate* **SR. ROBERT ANNE** *on the nice singing.* **REV. MOTHER** *enters from the right very excitedly muttering to herself followed by some other* **CHORUS MEMBERS.** *She is carrying a summons.)*

REV. MOTHER. This is a catastrophe!

FR. VIRGIL. What's the matter with you?

REV. MOTHER. This summons just came! That's what's the matter with me!

BR. TIMOTHY. Well, it can't be that bad.

REV. MOTHER. Oh, no? Take a look.

(She hands the summons to **BR. TIMOTHTY** *who then hands it to* **CHORUS MEMBER #1. REV. MOTHER** *continues walking stage left and to exit while saying:)*

C'mon, We've got to go pray for guidance. I should have just stayed with the circus!

*(***BR. TIMOTHY, FR. VIRGIL** *and* **SR. ROBERT ANNE** *follow* **REV. MOTHER** *and exit. The* **CHORUS** *crowds around the person with the summons. They see the summons and gasp!)*

(Director's Note: The following number is designed to be sung by the **CHORUS MEMBERS** *alone. However, depending on the size and skills of the* **CHORUS** *some of the principals can be included if deemed necessary.)*

[MUSIC NO. 19: CLEAN OUT THE FREEZER]

CHORUS MEMBER #1. *(looking at the summons)*
    WE'VE GOT TO CLEAN OUT THE FREEZER,
CHORUS MEMBERS #2, #3, #4.
    BY TOMORROW MORNING.
CHORUS MEMBERS #5, #6, #7.
    CAUSE THE JERSEY BOARD OF HEALTH
    HAS SENT THE FINAL WARNING.
CHORUS.
    THEY'RE NOT BUYING OUR LINE
    THAT DEAD NUNS RISE AND SHINE.
    WE MUST COMPLY OR FACE A FINE.

    WE'VE GOT TO CLEAN OUT THE FREEZER
    CAUSE THEY KNOW WE'RE THE ONES
    WHO HAVE REFUSED TO START DEFROSTING
    THOSE FOUR BLUE NUNS!
    THE TIME HAS COME TO SEND THEM OFF TO THEIR
        REWARD
    AND LET THEM GREET THE LORD!

    HEAVEN AWAITS!
    SO PACK 'EM IN CRATES
    AND TELL SAINT PETER

THEY'LL BE AT THOSE PEARLY GATES.
AND TELL HIM THESE ARE NUNS ON ICE
THAT WE'RE CERTAIN DIDN'T SIN,
AND WE'D BE VERY GRATEFUL
IF HE'D LET 'EM COME IN.

WE'VE GOT TO CLEAN OUT THE FREEZER
BY TOMORROW MORNIN'.
SOMEONE HOLLER TO GABRIEL
TO BLOW HIS HORN 'N'
WHEN THE SAINTS GO MARCHING
TO THAT HEAV'NLY DOOR
TELL 'EM THERE'S GONNA BE FOUR MORE!

WE'VE GOT TO CLEAN OUT THE FREEZER
AND DEFROST THE DEAD.
BECAUSE THE JERSELY BOARD OF HEALTH
IS CLAIMING THEY WERE MISLED.
THEY'RE NOT BUYING OUR LINE
THAT DEAD NUNS RISE AND SHINE.
WE MUST BURY THEM INSTEAD.
THEY'RE NOT BUYING OUR LINE –
NUNS RISE AND SHINE –
WE MUST BURY THEM INSTEAD!
THEY'RE DEAD!

(The **CHORUS** *exits chatting about the summons . The phone rings.* **SRS. HUBERT**, **ROBERT ANNE**, **AMNESIA** *and* **LEO** *enter from various spots. All holler "I'll get it" and start toward the phone with* **SR. LEO** *leading.* **REV. MOTHER** *has entered from the left to see what the commotion is about. At the stairs* **SR. LEO** *turns and says:)*

look @ phone

SR. LEO. I'll get it! I'm the novice!

(The others shrug their shoulders as **SR. LEO** *answers in her lowest sexiest voice.)*

Hello. Mount Saint Helen's.

REV. MOTHER. Well, who is it, Leo?

SR. LEO. It's Sister ~~Mary Wilhelm!~~ the hospital

(handwritten: hospital   look @ aud, horror hands to aud)

ALL. The nurse!

[MUSIC NO. 20: EUTHANASIA'S CHORD]

(The lights flicker à la grade-B horror movie.) *(handwritten: + to aud)*

SR. LEO. She says, Sister Julia, *(all cross themselves)* Child of God, was making her new chicken dish. Chicken with Correctol – or something like that. Anyway, it backfired! – She's in the hospital getting her stomach pumped.

REV. MOTHER. Oh, Lord deliver me. Is she coming over to do the show?

SR. LEO. *(into phone)* Is she coming over to do the show? *(To* **REV. MOTHER***)* No.

REV. MOTHER. No?

SR. LEO. No!

REV. MOTHER. Whoa!

SR. ROBERT ANNE. Oh! I can do my number!

REV. MOTHER. I don't think so!

*(***SR. LEO*** has hung up the phone and come back with the others.)*

Well, I'll just have to fill in for Sister Julia. Now let's see – I'll need her book – does anyone know what happened to her book?

SR. AMNESIA. Uh-oh. I forgot to bring it in. I left it in the station wagon.

REV. MOTHER. Well, I've got to have that book. Will one of you get it please?

(handwritten: everyone) **SRS. LEO, AMNESIA, & ROBERT ANNE.** I will!

REV. MOTHER. Alright, all of you go.

(handwritten: exit L) *(They all run off right.)*

[MUSIC NO. 22: JUST A COUPL'A SISTERS]

(handwritten: II iv) **REV. MOTHER.** Oh, Hubert. We've got sisters in the freezer, Marie Eugene's down at the Board of Health, and I don't know Julia's part. What's a Reverend Mother to do?!

SR. HUBERT.

EVERYTIME YOU HAVE TO FACE A CRISIS –
WHO'S THE ONE WHO HELPS YOU MUDDLE THROUGH?

REV. MOTHER.

ALRIGHT. I CONFESS IT. YES, THE TRUTH IS:
I COULDN'T DO IT WITHOUT YOU.
(to Conductor) Hit it!

BOTH.

WE'RE JUST A COUPL'A SISTERS
PLAIN AS WE CAN BE.
JUST A COUPL'A SISTERS
WHO'VE DISCOVERED HARMONY.

REV. MOTHER.

OH, SURE I COULD GO SOLO.

SR. HUBERT.

GOING SOLO CAN BE FUN.

BOTH.

BUT WHEN TWO SOLOS GET TOGETHER
THEY HARMONIZE AS ONE – NUN.
WE'RE JUST A COUPL'A SISTERS
OUT HERE HAVING FUN.

REV. MOTHER. *(to* **SR. HUBERT***)*

THE MISTRESS OF THE NOVICES,

SR. HUBERT. *(to* **REV. MOTHER***)*

AND REVEREND NUMBER ONE!

REV. MOTHER.

IT'S TRUE, I AM IN CHARGE HERE,
BUT I KNOW I'M NOT ALONE
AS LONG AS SISTER HUBERT
ADDS HER

BOTH.

HARMONIZING TONE.

SR. HUBERT.

I TRAIN ALL OUR NOVICES
AND DO IT ON MY OWN.
CAUSE I KNOW REVEREND MOTHER'S NEAR –
A STEPPING STONE.

REV. MOTHER. A stepping stone? A stepping stone to what, Hubert?

SR. HUBERT. Oh, Regina. It was just a rhyme. You see, the only other word I could think of was overgrown and I know how sensitive you are about your weight.

REV. MOTHER. Hubert! I'll have you know, I am not fat! I simply retain water.

SR. HUBERT. Ladies and gentlemen – Lake Superior!

(REV. MOTHER glares at SR. HUBERT who pulls them together.)

BOTH.
PUT US BOTH TOGETHER
AND WE'VE GOT IT ALL.

REV. MOTHER.
THE MELODY –

SR. HUBERT.
THE HARMONY –

BOTH.
SAINT PETER AND SAINT PAUL.

SR. HUBERT.
ALL WE NEED IS MARY
THEN WE'D HAVE A SINGING GROUP.

REV. MOTHER.
EVERY TOM AND DICK AND HARRY
IS A MARY IN THIS TROUPE!
Sister Mary Thomas,

SR. HUBERT.
SISTER MARY RICHARD,

REV. MOTHER.
SISTER MARY HAROLD,

SR. HUBERT.
SISTER MARYKNOLL.

BOTH.
SISTER MARY MARTIN, SISTER MARY PICKFORD,
SISTER MARY SUNSHINE. HEY, WE'RE ON A ROLL.
SISTER MARY HARTMAN, SISTER MARY ASTOR,

SR. HUBERT.

SISTER MERRY WIDOW –

REV. MOTHER.

SISTER, THAT'S ENOUGH!

SR. HUBERT.

SISTER MARY POPPINS, SISTER MERRY CHRISTMAS!

REV. MOTHER.

SISTER, THAT'S ENOUGH OF THIS "MARY" STUFF!

BOTH.

WE'RE JUST A COUPL'A SISTERS
IN WHAT YOU'D CALL "RARE FORM"
WHO'VE COME TO ENTERTAIN YOU
BY SINGING UP A STORM.
SWANEE, HOW I LOVE YA,

SR. HUBERT.

I LOVE REV'REND MAMMY!

BOTH.

WE'RE JUST A COUPL'A SISTERS,
PLAIN AS WE CAN BE.
JUST A COUPL'A SISTERS
WHO'VE DISCOVERED HARMONY!

(SR. HUBERT and REV. MOTHER exit right and return immediately on applause and bow. SR. AMNESIA quietly enters right carrying the cookbook which she places on the counter. She stands behind the counter. A second later SR. ROBERT ANNE enters on the platform and stops at the top of the stairs.)

REV. MOTHER. And now, ladies and gentlemen –   IIv

SR. ROBERT ANNE. *(interrupting)* Presenting – The Dying Nun!   sneak on SR

[MUSIC NO. 23: SOUP'S ON]

(SR. ROBERT ANNE comes down the stairs and exits left followed by SR. LEO wearing the "Sally Field-Flying-Nun hat" who comes center stage for her dance. REV. MOTHER and HUBERT look at each other in disbelief. REV. MOTHER goes to the bed and sits down. SR. HUBERT

sits at the counter. Since this piece was "unexpected" some **CHORUS** *people could also appear on the sidelines to see what it's all about. If there are "extras" watching they would leave as soon as the piece ends. "The Dying Nun Ballet" proceeds starring* **SR. LEO** *with support from* **SR. ROBERT ANNE** *who reappears with a hood over her head and a scythe as the Grim Reaper. At the end of the ballet* **REV. MOTHER** *rises from the bed.)*

scurry off

REV. MOTHER. Sister!

SR. LEO. Robert Anne said you'd think it was funny!

REV. MOTHER. Robert, I've about had it with you. One more time and you'll be the "dying nun!" *(pointing to* **SR. LEO***'s Flying Nun headgear)* Now get her outta that thing.

*(***SR. ROBERT ANNE*** *slams the two "wings" of the hat together atop* **SR. LEO***'s head. Now she looks like a sailboat.)*

SR. LEO. It was just a joke!

REV. MOTHER. Well, it wasn't funny. Who do you think you are? Sally Field?

SR. LEO. *(very indignantly)* Yes. And they liked me. They really liked me!

*(***SR. ROBERT ANNE*** *pulls* **SR. LEO** *offstage left before there's any more trouble.* **BR. TIMOTHY** *enters right and helps* **SR. AMNESIA** *move the counter to center stage as* **SR. HUBERT** *imitates* **SR. LEO** *dancing.* **BR. TIMOTHY** *then exits right. The Sisters take their places behind the counter.* **SR. HUBERT** *stage left,* **REV. MOTHER** *in the center, and* **SR. AMNESIA** *stage right.)*

REV. MOTHER. *(commenting on the dancing)* Hubert, stop that. She'll see you.

SR. HUBERT. Well, it was pretty funny.

REV. MOTHER. It wasn't. It's not enough that I've got to contend with Sister Robert Anne. Now, she's corrupting the novices.

(They put on aprons stored in the counter, while continuing the conversation.)

SR. HUBERT. You've always known she's a rebel.

REV. MOTHER. Well, it's not worth talking about. Besides, we've got something much more important to discuss. And I'm talking about the publication of this book – "Baking with the B.V.M."

SR. HUBERT. I think since some of the people in our audience may have brought non-Catholic friends we should explain that the B.V.M. is the Blessed Virgin Mary.

REV. MOTHER. I was just getting to that, Hubert. Thank-you very much!

*(**REV. MOTHER** ducks below the counter to put on a chef's hat. At the same time **SR. HUBERT** beats her breast three times, i.e. Mea Culpa, as if to say "Well, Excuuuuse me!" Then **REV. MOTHER** rises wearing the chef's hat. **SR. AMNESIA** is mesmerized and after a second speaks:)*

SR. AMNESIA. Reverend Mother, you look like the Pope!

SR. HUBERT. Hey, Regina. Do your Pope Benedict imitation.

REV. MOTHER. No…

SR. HUBERT. Oh, come on. You want to see it, don't you, folks?

REV. MOTHER. Oh, alright.

(She raises her hand and waves à la Queen Elizabeth, then tilts her head and starts snoring.)

REV. MOTHER. Enough…Well, now, folks, first of all, the book has a beautiful cover featuring a picture of our Blessed Mother in her cook's hat and apron. Wait till you see this. You're gonna love it. *(She shows the cover.)* So you see, when you're not using it for baking it makes a lovely devotional addition to your kitchen.

*(**SR. AMNESIA** is tugging on **REV. MOTHER**'s sleeve.)*

REV. MOTHER. I know, dear. Sister Amnesia has designed a terrific wooden stand for the book.

(SR. AMNESIA gets a wooden stand from under the counter and proudly places it on the counter. It is a disaster. REV. MOTHER is stunned.)

Did you make that?

(SR. AMNESIA nods proudly, "yes.")

(REV. MOTHER turns to SR. HUBERT) She made that. *(to SR. AMNESIA)* All by yourself?

(Again SR. AMNESIA nods.)

(to SR. HUBERT) All by herself. Nice house –

SR. HUBERT & REV. MOTHER. Nobody home!

REV. MOTHER. *(pointing upward to the right)* Look, Amnesia. An angel!

(SR. AMNESIA steps out from behind the counter looking up in the air as REV. MOTHER grabs the wooden stand and tosses it behind the counter. SR. AMNESIA steps back and before she can say that she didn't see the angel REV. MOTHER continues.)

Flew in, flew out! *(indicating the countertop)* Look, all clean. Well, shall we take a look at the book?

SR. HUBERT. Why not?

SR. JULIA. Wait, I'm here!

(SR. JULIA enters left pulling an IV on a rolling stand along with her. SR. WILHELM Is following her.)

REV. MOTHER. *(looking up to heaven)* Why me, Lord?

SR. WILHELM. I tried to stop her.

REV. MOTHER. Ladies and gentlemen, "Baking with the B.V.M." by Sister Julia *(all cross themselves)* Child of God.

(SR. JULIA talkes the chef's hat off REV. MOTHER's head and puts it on. REV. MOTHER and SR. WILHELM exit left as SR. JULIA takes REV. MOTHER's place.)

SR. JULIA. Well, shall we take a look at the book?

SR. HUBERT. Why stop now?

(**SR. JULIA** *opens the book. All "oooh" with delight.*)

(*Director's Note: From here down to Music Cue 24 the script can be printed in the prop cookbook eliminating the need for memorization!*)

SR. JULIA. You will see that the Main Section is just chock full of unusual recipes especially suited to the Catholic Kitchen. For example – Here's Cesar Franck's Panis Angelicus. A delightful taste treat consisting of two hot dogs, wrapped in anchovies and served on a slice of Angel Food cake!

SR. HUBERT. *(looking horrified)* Have you ever tested this stuff?

SR. JULIA. Well, I can't do everything you know. I've got to cook the meals, buy the food –

SR. HUBERT. How could you not check this out, after what's already happened –

(*The two began arguing simultaneously. Argument escalates until we hear* **SR. HUBERT** *say:*)

SR. HUBERT. You said you were going to test everything the day we were watching the Food Channel and that Iron Chef got Chopped!

SR. JULIA. Well, it's too late now, isn't it?

SR. HUBERT. In a word, yes!

SR. JULIA. Well, we'll just go on. Look, this one's really cute. The Mortally sinful Devil's Food Cake.

SR. AMNESIA. If you eat that, you'll go to hell.

SR. JULIA. Yeah, but what a way to go!

SR. HUBERT. Here's one. Mary Magdalene Tarts! I'll bet they're easy!

SR. JULIA. And cheap! *(they both laugh at their own jokes)*

SR. AMNESIA. Look. Here's a recipe for Boy Scouts.

SR. JULIA. Why don't you read that one, Amnesia? *(taking the book,* **SR. AMNESIA** *starts reading silently)* Out loud, Sister.

SR. AMNESIA. Oh. "Boy Scout Treats." It says, "First, get twelve brownies real hot!"

(**SR. JULIA** *pulls the book back. She and* **SR. HUBERT** *look down into the book and then to each other.* **SR. JULIA** *rips the page out, and continues.*)

SR. JULIA. It's a misprint!

SR. HUBERT. Now, this looks pretty good.

SR. JULIA. Oh yes, my "Turkey Stuffing."
You take one package of regular stuffing mix.

SR. HUBERT. One package, regular stuffing mix.

SR. JULIA. One onion, minced.

SR. HUBERT. One onion.

SR. JULIA. One cup of unpopped popcorn.

SR. HUBERT. Unpopped popcorn.

SR. JULIA. Mix it all together.

SR. HUBERT. Mix together.

SR. JULIA. Stuff it in your bird.

SR. HUBERT. Stuff it in your bird.

SR. JULIA. Put your bird in the oven.

SR. HUBERT. Bird in the oven.

SR. JULIA. 400 degrees.

SR. HUBERT. 400 degrees.

SR. JULIA. *(turns page)* And when his ass blows off he's done!

(**SR. JULIA** *thinks this is very amusing while* **SR. HUBERT** *is horrified. The two continue to look at each other and the book until laughter peaks.*)

SR. HUBERT. Holy Smoke!

(**SR. HUBERT** *is pointing to the book.* **SRS. LEO, ROBERT ANNE,** *and* **REV. MOTHER** *enter left.* **SRS. BRENDAN, LUKE** *and* **BR. TIMOTHY** *enter right.*)

SR. ROBERT ANNE. What's the matter? Is something burning?

SR. HUBERT. No, she's included the recipe for that soup.

ALL BUT SR. JULIA. What?

SR. BRENDAN. Look, it's right here – vichyssoise soup.

SR. JULIA. Well, the recipe isn't poison.

REV. MOTHER. How do you know? I should have known better than to trust you! We certainly can't sell this thing.

SR. JULIA. Fine. That's the thanks I get.

(**SR. JULIA** *takes the cookbook and starts exiting left with the IV trailing along.*)

And the next time the Monsignor comes over you can press your own cluckin' duck.

REV. MOTHER. For your information ducks don't cluck, they quack!

SR. LUKE. Speaking of quacks, now what are you going to do? You were counting on the books to bring in some extra money.

[MUSIC NO. 24: SECOND FIDDLE (REPRISE)]

SR. LEO. I could do my fire baton.

SR. BRENDAN. No fire baton!

SR. AMNESIA. I could do my bird calls.

REV. MOTHER. And what, dare I ask, are your bird calls?

SR. AMNESIA. Here, birdie, birdie. Here, birdie, birdie.

SR. ROBERT ANNE. I don't believe this!

REV. MOTHER. What?

SR. ROBERT ANNE.

I'M CAUGHT IN THE MIDDLE
STILL PLAYING SECOND FIDDLE
WHILE YOU PEDDLE POISON RECIPES.
YOU COMPLETELY DISREGARD
THAT I'VE WORKED VERY HARD
ON A SONG –

REV. MOTHER. Well, sing it, please!

SR. ROBERT ANNE. Do you really mean it?

REV. MOTHER. Yes. Do it before I change my mind.

(SR. ROBERT ANNE goes up toward the band area as if to talk to FR. PATRICK, the conductor. SRS. LEO & AMNESIA exit right. SRS. BRENDAN & LUKE exit left. BR. TIMOTHY puts the counter back in place on stage right and exits.)

take bar off SR

(heading to the left exit) Good Lord, I feel like I'm back in the Leper Colony the way things are falling to pieces around here.

SR. HUBERT. *(following REV. MOTHER)* How could Julia be so stupid?

REV. MOTHER. How could I be so stupid? *(She exits left.)*

SR. HUBERT. *(turning to audience)* Let me count the ways. *(She exits left.)*

(SR. ROBERT ANNE moves downstage center.)

[MUSIC NO. 25: I JUST WANT TO BE A STAR]

SR. ROBERT ANNE.
WHEN I BECAME A NUN
AT A VERY EARLY AGE,
I HAD TO CHOOSE BETWEEN THE CONVENT
AND A LIFE UPON THE STAGE.
SO WHEN REVEREND MOTHER SAID,
"WE'RE PUTTIN' ON A SHOW,"
I MUST TELL YOU, I WAS THRILLED TO DEATH.
I COULDN'T WAIT TO GO.

WELL, NOW TO MY SURPRISE
REVEREND MOTHER DIDN'T SEE
WHAT'S SO OBVIOUS.
THE STAGE IS MEANT FOR ME.
MONEY AND FAME,
I DON'T DESIRE.
I ONLY WANT TO SPARKLE
I'M NOT HERE TO START A FIRE!

I DON'T CARE IF I'M EVER RICH OR FAMOUS
I JUST WANT TO BE A STAR.

I DON'T CARE IF YOU KNOW WHAT MY NAME IS *(ROBERT!)*,
I JUST WANT TO BE A STAR.

I WANT TO BE
THE NUN WHO MAKES YOU CHEER.
THE NUN WHO'S OUT IN FRONT
INSTEAD OF AT THE REAR.
FOR ONCE, I WANT
TO LEAD THE BAND
AND HAVE THE CROWD
IN THE PALM OF MY HAND.

I DON'T CARE IF I'M EVER RICH OR FAMOUS,
I JUST WANT TO BE A STAR!

WHEN WE BEGAN THIS SHOW,
THEY WERE REALLY GREEN.
THEY DIDN'T KNOW A CHORUS LINE
FROM A CHORUS QUEEN.

THEY DIDN'T REALIZE
THAT IN THE CHORUS LINE
YOU NEVER GET TO STRUT YOUR STUFF,
YOU NEVER REALLY SHINE!
I DON'T CARE IF I'M EVER RICH OR FAMOUS,
I JUST WANT TO BE A STAR.
SURE, IT'S TRUE. MY ONLY CLAIM TO FAME IS,
"I GOT WHAT IT TAKES TO BE A STAR!"

I KNOW MY VOW OF POVERTY
SAYS I CAN'T MAKE A FORTUNE,
BUT WHEN WE'RE EIGHTY
AND SETTIN' ON THE PORCH IN
THE OLD NUNS' HOME,
AND THEY ASK WHO WE ARE
I JUST WANT TO SAY:
"HEY! I WAS A STAR!"

*(Several **CHORUS NUNS** enter right wearing feather headdresses and carrying a long boa which they place over **SR. ROBERT ANNE**'s shoulders. They stay on stage as "back-up" dancers.)*

SR. ROBERT ANNE.
> I DON'T CARE IF I'M EVER RICH OR FAMOUS,
> JUST SO I CAN BE –
> THE CHORUS LINE IS NOT FOR ME –
> I'M RED HOT TO BE A STAR.
> YO! REGINA! PARK YOUR OWN DAMN CAR.

> (**SR. ROBERT ANNE** *throws the car keys off stage right.*
> *The* **CHORUS** *is shocked and hurries off stage left.*)

> I JUST WANNA BE A STAR!

> *[MUSIC NO. 25A: STAR PLAYOFF]*

> (**SR. ROBERT ANNE** *is strutting around the stage and*
> *comes downstage left and is teasing a man with her boa.*
> **REV. MOTHER** *comes onstage from the right followed by*
> **SRS. AMNESIA** *and* **LEO** *who "hang" upstage. When*
> **REV. MOTHER** *gets to* **SR. ROBERT ANNE** *she shakes*
> *the keys at her.* **SR. ROBERT ANNE** *takes the keys and*
> **REV. MOTHER** *takes the boa.* **SR. ROBERT ANNE** *stands*
> *shamefully silent.*)

REV. MOTHER. *(addressing audience member)* You're no help at all! *(to* **SR. ROBERT ANNE***)* Well, our little sparkler turned out to be quite a firecracker!

SR. ROBERT ANNE. *(sincerely)* I'm sorry, Reverend Mother.

REV. MOTHER. Well, that was quite a surprise, Robert. You were sensational!

SR. ROBERT ANNE. I was?!

REV. MOTHER. Yes, you were.

> (**REV. MOTHER** *extends her hand and as they start to*
> *shake hands* **REV. MOTHER** *speaks:*)

> That'll be six Our Fathers and seven hundred Hail Marys!

> (*She then sends* **SR. ROBERT ANNE** *to the center stage*
> *area to join* **SRS. AMNESIA** *and* **LEO** *who also move*
> *center.*)

> And now, ladies and gentlemen, we'd like to present our version of –

(Each puts on an army hat as her name is mentioned. **SR. ROBERT ANNE** *is waving at the audience member.)*

– Patty – Maxine – and Laverne – the Saint Andrews Sisters of Hoboken in a number they've prepared especially for this evening.

*(***REV. MOTHER*** *starts offstage left and catches* **SR. ROBERT ANNE**.*)*

Robert! Leave that man alone!

*(***REV. MOTHER*** *continues off left "working the boa" and before she is offstage turns back one more time and reprimands the audience member.)*

I'm watching you!

(When **REV. MOTHER** *is off,* **SR. ROBERT ANNE** *turns to cue* **FR. PATRICK**.*)*

[MUSIC NO. 26: THE DRIVE-IN]

ALL THREE.

> IT SEEMS LIKE ONLY YESTERDAY
> WHEN LIFE WAS QUITE SERENE.
> THE DAYS WERE RATHER UNEVENTFUL,
> WHAT YOU'D CALL ROUTINE.
>
> THEN CAME THAT FATAL NIGHT
> WHEN JULIA MADE HER VICHYSSOISE.
> FOR FIFTY-TWO, "BON APPETIT"
> WAS ALSO "BON VOYAGE."
>
> THEN OUR TRANQUIL LIFE WAS OVER
> FOR WE KNEW WHAT WE MUST DO.
> WE HAD TO RAISE THE MONEY
> TO INTER THE FIFTY-TWO!
>
> AT TIMES IT ALL SEEMED HOPELESS
> AND MUCH MORE THAN WE COULD BEAR.
> WE WOULD ALL HAVE LOST OUR MINDS
> HAD WE NOT STOPPED – AH –

SR. ROBERT ANNE.

> TO GO TO THE DRIVE-IN,

[handwritten annotation: BRIGHTEN TONE / More Sutton Foster / a la Anything Goes]

SR. AMNESIA.

AT THE SKYLINE DRIVE-IN,

SRS. LEO & ROBERT ANNE.

DRIVE-IN,

SR. LEO.

WE CAN ALWAYS SURVIVE IN.

SRS. AMNESIA & ROBERT ANNE.

WE SURVIVE IN,

ALL THREE.

TIMES OF STRESS AND STRAIN.

DOO DOO BEE DOO BEE DOO
DOO DOO BEE DOO BEE DOO
DOO DOO BEE DOO BEE DOO WAH! *BIG FALL*

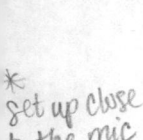

GIVE YOURSELF A CHANGE OF SCENE
BY ALTERING THE DAY'S ROUTINE.
FIND THE NEAREST MOVIE SCREEN
AND LET YOURSELF GO.
IT'S BETTER THAN A MAGAZINE
OF COURSE, YOU'LL WANT TO KEEP IT CLEAN.
BUT IF IT'S A BIT OBSCENE,
WHO'LL EVER KNOW?

THAT YOU'VE BEEN TO THE DRIVE-IN.
HEY, WHEN YOU ARRIVE,
FIND A PLACE TO PARK AND DIVE IN
TO A BOX OF BUTTERED POPCORN AND REVIVE YOURSELF.
YOUR SPIRITS COME ALIVE WHEN
YOU DON'T HAVE TO CONNIVE.
THERE ISN'T A RIVAL
WHEN A DRIVE'LL MEAN SURVIVAL.

* set up close to the mic

SR. LEO.

AS SOON AS YOU ARRIVE IN,

SRS. AMNESIA & ROBERT ANNE.

YOU ARRIVE IN,

SR. AMNESIA.

THE SKYLINE DRIVE-IN,

SRS. LEO & ROBERT ANNE.

DRIVE-IN.

SR. AMNESIA.

> IT'S THE ONE PLACE I'VE BEEN,

SRS. LEO & ROBERT ANNE.

> ONE PLACE I'VE BEEN

ALL THREE.

> THAT'LL CHASE THE BLUES AWAY.

> *(The three go to the counter as* **SRS. LUKE** *and* **BRENDAN** *enter right as "ushers" and bring it center stage turning it around to reveal the back end of the "Grease" car.)*

> ENOUGH BALLYHOO ABOUT WHAT TO DO.
> IT'S TIME TO ROLL OUR HOMEMADE CONVENT FILM
>   DISPLAY.
> SCIDDLY-AH-DOO-BEE-DOO-WAH-WAH-WAH!

[MUSIC NO. 27: NUNSMOKE]

> *(The three face upstage and sit. The "ushers" stand at either side. The lights go to blue.)*

SR. ROBERT ANNE. Bring in the movie screen! *(nothing happens)* I said, bring in the movie screen!

FR. PATRICK. *(looking upward)* It won't come down.

SR. LUKE. It looks like it's stuck.

SR. BRENDAN. It was fine at play practice.

FR. PATRICK. Well, it's not fine now.

SR. ROBERT ANNE. Oh, for Pete's sakes. C'mon, guys. Let's go try to fix it.

*(***SRS. ROBERT ANNE, BRENDAN, LUKE** *&* **LEO** *exit left while* **SR. AMNESIA** *has slipped down behind the lunch counter. As the lights come up, she peeks her head up above the counter.)*

SR. AMNESIA. I don't think that was supposed to happen. *(hollering toward offstage right)* Brother Tim, can you come out here?

*(***BR. TIMOTHY** *enters right.)*

I don't think that was supposed to happen.

BR. TIMOTHY. I know.

(The two continue talking as they put the counter back on stage right.)

SR. AMNESIA. So, what do I do now?

BR. TIMOTHY. Why don't you tell 'em one of your stories?

SR. AMNESIA. Oh, they don't want to hear one of my stories.

BR. TIMOTHY. Sure, they do. *(He leads audience applause.)*

SR. AMNESIA. Oh, they do! Do you remember that story I was telling you last week?

BR. TIMOTHY. Yeah. That was a good one. Do you remember it?

SR. AMNESIA. Yeah, I think so. *(turning to audience)* Okay. I'm gonna tell you a story. It's about me.

*(**BR. TIMOTHY** exits right giving her a "thumbs up." She pulls the bed out and lies down revealing a large L and R on the bottom of her shoes.)*

[MUSIC NO. 28: I COULD HAVE GONE TO NASHVILLE]

SOMETIMES IN THE MORNING
BEFORE THE FIRST BELL RINGS,
I LIE HERE WIDE AWAKE
WONDERIN' ALL KINDS OF THINGS.

(She sits up.)

LIKE WHO I AM, OR WHAT I'D BE
IF I WERE NOT A NUN.
I SUPPOSE I COULD BE ANYTHING
BUT IF I COULD BE ANYONE –

(She gets up off the bed.)

I'D LIKE TO BE COUNTRY SINGER
LIKE LORETTA LYNN.
WITH A DELUXE WINNEBAGO
THAT I COULD TRAVEL IN.

SR. AMNESIA.

I'D HAVE WIGS LIKE DOLLY PARTON
I MIGHT EVEN PIERCE MY EARS.
I'D HAVE RHINESTONE STUDDED COWBOY BOOTS
AND A SEQUINED GOWN FROM SEARS.

I'D HAVE ME SOME BACK UP SINGERS,

(Wearing "Dolly Parton" blonde wigs, a few **CHORUS MEMBERS** *stick their heads out from various places, sing a couple of back-up lines and then disappear.)*

AND A REAL LIVE BLUEGRASS BAND.
AND I WOULD GO TO NASHVILLE
AND APPEAR AT OPRYLAND.

I'D SING SONGS OF INSPIRATION.
I'D SING SONGS IN TIME OF STRIFE.
SONGS LIKE "DROP KICK ME, JESUS,
THROUGH THE GOAL POST OF LIFE!"

Wait a minute – wait a minute. It's all comin' back to me – I was going to be a country singer. And there was a contest – a big contest – and I remember walking out on this huge stage –

AND WHEN THEY TURNED UP THAT SPOTLIGHT
ALL THAT GLITTERED THERE WAS ME.
PEOPLE ALL WERE SAYING,
"SHE'S ANOTHER BRENDA LEE!"

OH, I COULD'VE GONE TO NASHVILLE
AND BECOME A COUNTRY STAR.
BUT SOMETHING DEEP INSIDE OF ME
WAS CALLING FROM AFAR.

(She moves back toward the bed.)

I STARTED MY NEW LIFE
INSIDE THE CONVENT WALL.
BRENDA LEE HAD GIVEN WAY
TO SISTER MARY *(She pauses.)* – PAUL –
SISTER MARY PAUL
– Sister Mary Paul – that's it!

(She jumps up on the bed.)

SR. AMNESIA.

I'm Sister Mary Paul!

I REMEMBER IT ALL –

OH, I COULD'VE GONE TO NASHVILLE
AND BECOME LORETTA LYNN
BUT SOMETHING MUCH MORE POWERFUL
WAS CALLING FROM WITHIN.

OH, I COULD'VE GONE TO NASHVILLE
BUT I CAME HERE THAT DAY.

(She kneels on the bed and the lights come down to a pinspot on her face.)

I MUST SAY A LITTLE THANK-YOU PRAYER
THAT IT ALL TURNED OUT THIS WAY. AMEN.

[MUSIC NO. 28A: NASHVILLE PLAYOFF]

(Blackout. Lights up. **SR. AMNESIA** *is jumping on the bed.)*

Come out here, everybody. I remember who I am. Hurry. I remember who I am!

(THE ENTIRE COMPANY, *including* **SR. JULIA,** *without the IV, come onstage from various entrances.* **REV. MOTHER** *comes to the side of the bed.)*

REV. MOTHER. Well, who are you?

SR. AMNESIA. I was going to be a country singer and I was going to Nashville, but I felt I had this calling and so I decided not to become a big star and I became unimportant like all of you!

(The Sisters do a "take" to each other.)

I'm Sister Mary Paul!

(REV. MOTHER *helps* **SR. AMNESIA** *off the bed.)*

SR. LEO. Sister Mary Paul! That's a nice name. Isn't it, Hubert?

(BR. TIMOTHY *puts the bed back.)*

REV. MOTHER. You know I remember hearing about a Sister Mary Paul when we were in France, but when we came back here no one knew what happened to her – and then you mysteriously appeared and all you could tell us was that a crucifix hit you on the head. So you're Sister Mary Paul.

*(***REV. MOTHER*** *steps aside "in thought" as* **SR. ROBERT ANNE** *motions for* **SR. AMNESIA** *to come to her.)*

SR. ROBERT ANNE. Do you remember everything?

SR. AMNESIA. Well, I think so. You see, I won this contest, and I was going –

REV. MOTHER. *(very excitedly)* Contest. Oh, my heavens! That's it!

ALL BUT REV. MOTHER. What?

REV. MOTHER. Sister Mary Paul was the name of the nun who won the Publishers Clearing House Sweepstakes and they could never find her. *(to* **SR. AMNESIA***)* That's you! We've got the money! Saints be praised! We're rich!

[MUSIC NO. 29: GLORIA IN EXCELSIS DEO]

ALL.

GLORIA IN EXCELSIS DEO!

SR. HUBERT. Somebody call the Prize Patrol!

SR. JULIA. This means we can bury the last four dead sisters.

SR. ROBERT ANNE. And get a Tivo for the Plasma TV.

SR. AMNESIA. *(à la Shake 'n' Bake commercial)* And I helped!

REV. MOTHER. You certainly did, dear. You know, I was really starting to get worried about having to defrost those girls tomorrow morning.

FR. VIRGIL. It just goes to show that the Lord does, indeed, work in mysterious ways.

SR. LUKE. One minute we're desperate –

SR. BRENDAN. The next minute we're rich.

SR. WILHELM. You just never know what the Almighty has planned.

SR. HUBERT. Today, the Mistress of Novices, tomorrow –

SR. LEO. *(interrupting)* Tomorrow, the world could be saluting the first "nun ballerina."

REV. MOTHER. Of course, dear – and I'll be a size five! *(to audience)* The important thing is that we can send those last four sisters off to their heavenly reward. And we can get back to concentrating on our own heavenly rewards. Because after all, each and everyone of us here has the potential to become a saint!

SR. HUBERT. And you know something?

REV. MOTHER. What?

[MUSIC NO. 30: HOLIER THAN THOU]

SR. HUBERT.
IT'S NOT THAT HARD TO BE A SAINT.
ALL YOU HAVE TO DO
IS PICK A SAINT TO EMULATE
WHO MOST EMBODIES YOU.

THEN FIGURE OUT WHAT MADE THAT SAINT
THE IDOL OF TODAY.
THEN FOLLOW IN THOSE FOOTSTEPS
AND YOU'LL EARN THE RIGHT TO SAY:

REV. MOTHER. Look out, girls. She's got the spirit!

(Everyone backs away giving **SR. HUBERT** *center stage.)*

SR. HUBERT.
I'M HOLIER THAN THOU.
I'VE GOT THE SPIRIT NOW.
I FEEL LIKE I'M IN HEAVEN
CAUSE I'M HOLIER THAN THOU.

I'M HOLIER THAN THOU.
I'VE GOT THE SPIRIT NOW.
I THANK GOD ALMIGHTY
THAT I'M HOLIER THAN THOU.
Alright. See how easy it is? Somebody, pick a saint.

SR. AMNESIA. Saint Bernadette!

SR. HUBERT. That's an excellent choice, Sister.
BERNADETTE OF LOURDES
CAN BE EASILY ACHIEVED.
SHE SAID SHE SAW A VIRGIN
WHICH, OF COURSE, NO ONE BELIEVED.
PEOPLE SAID SHE'D LOST HER MIND,
THERE WAS NO LADY THERE.
SO GO AND FIND A VIRGIN
THEN COME BACK HERE AND DECLARE:

I'M HOLIER THAN THOU.
I'VE GOT THE SPIRIT NOW.
I FEEL LIKE I'M IN HEAVEN
CAUSE I'M HOLIER THAN THOU.

I'M HOLIER THAN THOU.
I'VE GOT THE SPIRIT NOW.
I THANK GOD ALMIGHTY
THAT I'M HOLIER THAN THOU.
Alright, can you help me out?

ALL BUT SR. HUBERT.
DOOT, DOOT, DOO. DOOT, DOOT, DOO.
DOOT, DOOT, DOO. DOOT, DOOT, DOO.

SR. HUBERT. That's it. Let's have another.

SR. ROBERT ANNE. Saint Lucy! I love Lucy!

SR. HUBERT.
LUCY WAS A VIRGIN
SO IF THAT TEST YOU DON'T FAIL.
LUCY COULD BE PERFECT
EXCEPT FOR ONE DETAIL.

LUCY WAS A MARTYR
WHICH COULD BE A BIT SEVERE.

SR. JULIA.
I THINK I'LL PICK A LIVING SAINT
AND STICK AROUND TO HEAR:

I'M HOLIER THAN THOU.

SR. HUBERT. Preach!

SR. JULIA & REV. MOTHER.
> I'VE GOT THE SPIRIT NOW.
> I FEEL LIKE I'M IN HEAVEN
> CAUSE I'M HOLIER THAN THOU.
> SR. JULIA, REV. MOTHER & SR. HUBERT
> I'M HOLIER THAN THOU.
> I'VE GOT THE SPIRIT NOW.
> I THANK GOD ALMIGHTY
> THAT I'M HOLIER THAN THOU.

ALL BUT SR. HUBERT.
> DOOT, DOOT, DOO. DOOT, DOOT, DOO.
> DOOT, DOOT, DOO. DOOT, DOOT, DOO.

SR. HUBERT. Alright, good people. There's something else I want to tell you.

> YOU CAN BE SAINT ANTHONY
> AND RUN A "LOST AND FOUND."
> IF YOU'RE INTO TORTURE
> SAINT AGNES WAS RENOWNED.

> MARY MAGDALENE IS PERFECT
> FOR THE HOOKER WITH A DREAM.
> WITH GOD ALL THINGS ARE POSSIBLE
> NOTHING'S TOO EXTREME. SING!

ALL BUT SR. HUBERT.
> I'M HOLIER THAN THOU.
> I'M HOLIER THAN THOU.
> I'M HOLIER THAN THOU.
> I'M HOLIER THAN THOU.

(handwritten in margin: BIG so that we need to go now)

SR. HUBERT. Alright, let's bring it down. Bring it down.

(Back-up singing continues softly.)

(handwritten in margin: Respond to Daniel re:)

Listen to me now, good people. When you leave here tonight *(today)* we want you to go home and pick a saint – So that you can get dowwwwwwwn! – To get uuuuuuuuup! – And get out on that road to heaven! Alright, put your hands together!

(SR. HUBERT *leads hand-clapping.)*

Now, can I get an "A-men?"

ALL BUT SR. HUBERT. A-men!

SR. HUBERT. A-men!

ALL BUT SR. HUBERT. A-men!

SR. HUBERT. A-A-men!

ALL BUT SR. HUBERT. A-A-men!

SR. HUBERT. A-A-men!

ALL BUT SR. HUBERT. A-A-men!

ALL.

> I'M HOLIER THAN THOU.
> I'VE GOT THE SPIRIT NOW.
> I FEEL LIKE I'M IN HEAVEN
> CAUSE I'M HOLIER THAN THOU.

> I'M HOLIER THAN THOU.
> I'VE GOT THE SPIRIT NOW.
> I THANK GOD ALMIGHTY
> THAT I'M HOLIER THAN THOU.

[handwritten: speak instead of sing charity lots of ups & down]

SR. HUBERT. One more time!

ALL.

> I'M HOLIER THAN THOU.
> I'VE GOT THE SPIRIT NOW.
> I FEEL LIKE I'M IN HEAVEN
> CAUSE I'M HOLIER THAN THOU.

> I'M HOLIER THAN THOU.
> I'VE GOT THE SPIRIT NOOOOOOOOOWWWWW.

[handwritten: out of breath, AMEN wipe brow, etc. ENERGY!]

SR. HUBERT.

> I FEEL LIKE I'M IN HEAVEN –

> (**SR. HUBERT** *riffs as we hear the others shouting such things as "Praise the Lord," "Sing it, Sister," etc.)*

> I SAID, I FEEL LIKE I'M IN HEAVEN –

SR. ROBERT ANNE. Why, Sister? Why?

SR. HUBERT.

> BECAUSE –

ALL BUT SR. HUBERT. Why?

[handwritten: on second "bump"]

SR. HUBERT.

> BECAUSE –

ALL BUT SR. HUBERT. Why?

SR. HUBERT.

    BECAUSE I AM HOLIER –

    THAAAAAAAAAAANNNNN

SR. HUBERT ALL BUT SR. HUBERT.

    THOU! I'M HOLIER THAN THOU,

    I'M HOLIER THAN THOU,

    I'M HOLIER THAN THOU,

ALL.

    HOLIER THAN THOU! YOW!

    [MUSIC NO. 31: NUNSENSE (REPRISE)]

ALL.

    TURN UP THE SPOTLIGHT,

    CAUSE WHEN WE GOT LIGHT

    ALL THAT WE CAN SAY IS

    "IT REALLY HAS BEEN FUN,

    THANK-YOU EACH AND EVERYONE."

    IT'S TIME TO END OUR PLAY!

    BY THE WAY,

    GOD BLESS YOU EACH DAY!"

    [MUSIC NO. 32: BOWS & EXIT MUSIC]

End Act Two

COSTUME PLOT

The nuns wear the habit of the Little Sisters of Hoboken consisting of:

Black tights

Long sleeve black t-shirt

Black orthopedic oxford shoes

Black tunic with breast pocket

Black belt buckled in the back

Rosary hung from the left side of the belt

Black scapular

White guimpe (bib collar)

White wimple (headpiece)

Black veil lined with white. (The novice, SR. MARY LEO, wears an all-white veil.)

FR. VIRGIL and BR. TIMOTHY wear Franciscan brown robes with brown cowls and a white "cincture" cord as a belt.

SR. WILHELM, the nurse, can wear an all-white habit or just a large "red cross symbol" on her scapular and SR. JULIA, CHILD OF GOD can wear an identifying apron.

REV. MOTHER wears a crucifix that hangs just below the white collar. The cord on the crucifix goes under the collar.

If glasses are worn they should be of plain design and the arms of the glasses go inside the wimple.

Students should be in school uniforms.

Chorus nuns can be in full habits with black or white veils, and some can be postulants in shorter black dresses with off-the-face veils.

Chorus priests and brothers can be in black cassocks (simple black robe) or in black pants and black shirts with Roman collars.

To see a demonstration of the nun's habit, visit Youtube and search "A Nunsense Lesson." Habits and some props are available for purchase or rent from Nunsense, Inc. at www.nunsense.com. Phone 1-800-YES-NUNS.

SET PROPS

PROP	LOCATION
Statues of Mary & Joseph	Either side of the proscenium
Flag on floor stand	Next to statue of St. Joseph
"Grease" Logo	Hung upstage
School Bell (Electric/ Practical)	Mounted on upstage wall
Juke Box (or Record player)	Upstage center
Small stool	Next to juke box
Lunch counter on rolling platform with three or four low stools (18" high) and hidden shelf in back. The back of the counter needs to have a half door that drops down to reveal the shelf. When closed the back looks like the rear end of the "Grease" car.	Downstage right
Tray with Ketchup, Mustard, Salt, Pepper, etc. to dress counter top	On lunch counter top (*Need to be removed at intermission*)
Three aprons, One adjustable chef's hat, One homemade very crooked, wooden book stand	Pre-set on shelf in lunch counter
Easel with poster announcing **Welcome** **"Little Sisters of Hoboken"** **Benefit Performance**	Center stage
Large poster of Marilyn Monroe in a swimsuit with Velcro tabs at waist for attaching skirt.	Hung upstage left
Large poster of James Dean or other Star performer	Hung upstage right
Black or Plaid "skirt" that looks like bunting with two Velcro tabs for attaching to Marilyn poster.	Draped on easel.
Bed with spread and pillows	Downstage left
Set of lockers	Stage right
Wall phone or pay phone	Mounted on upper platform wall

HAND PROPS

Quiz questions on 3 x 5 cards (Sr. Amnesia)
3 Prizes per performance (Sr. Amnesia)
Bathrobe (Sr. Leo)
Toe shoes (Sr. Leo)
Fuzzy slippers to go over toe shoes (Sr. Leo)
Iron (Sr. Julia)
Lilacs with gift card (Sr. Leo)
Funnel with elastic (Sr. Robert Anne)
Small paper bag with "Rush" bottle inside (Sr. Robert Anne)
Chef's hat (Sr. Robert Anne)
Automatic umbrella (Rev. Mother)
"Dying Nun" hat à la Sally Field (Sr. Leo)
"Grim Reaper" black hood and scythe
"Sister Mary Annette" puppet (Sr. Amnesia)
Plastic fruit hung on a circle of wire to make a "fruit crown"
    (Sr. Robert Anne)
Small book entitled "The Understudy" (Sr. Robert Anne)
Maracas (Sr. Robert Anne)
Shopping bag, weighted to simulate shoes inside (Sr. Hubert)
Summons from Jersey Board of Health (Rev. Mother)
"Baking with the B.V.M." Cookbook (Sr. Amnesia)
IV bag on a rolling pole (Sr. Julia, Child of God)
Red feather headdresses (Chorus Dancers)
1 long red boa (Sr. Robert Anne)
3 "Andrews Sisters" Army hats

In one of the lockers on stage right:
Wooden ruler on a belt clip (Sr. Amnesia)

In appropriate dressing rooms:
"Clicker" (Rev. Mother)
Keys on a removable belt strap (Sr. Robert Anne)

Set Design

Set Design

Close up of stool, jukebox, and trash can

Front of lunch counter
*Photos courtesy of author

Set Design

Back of lunch counter
*Photo courtesy of author

Set Design

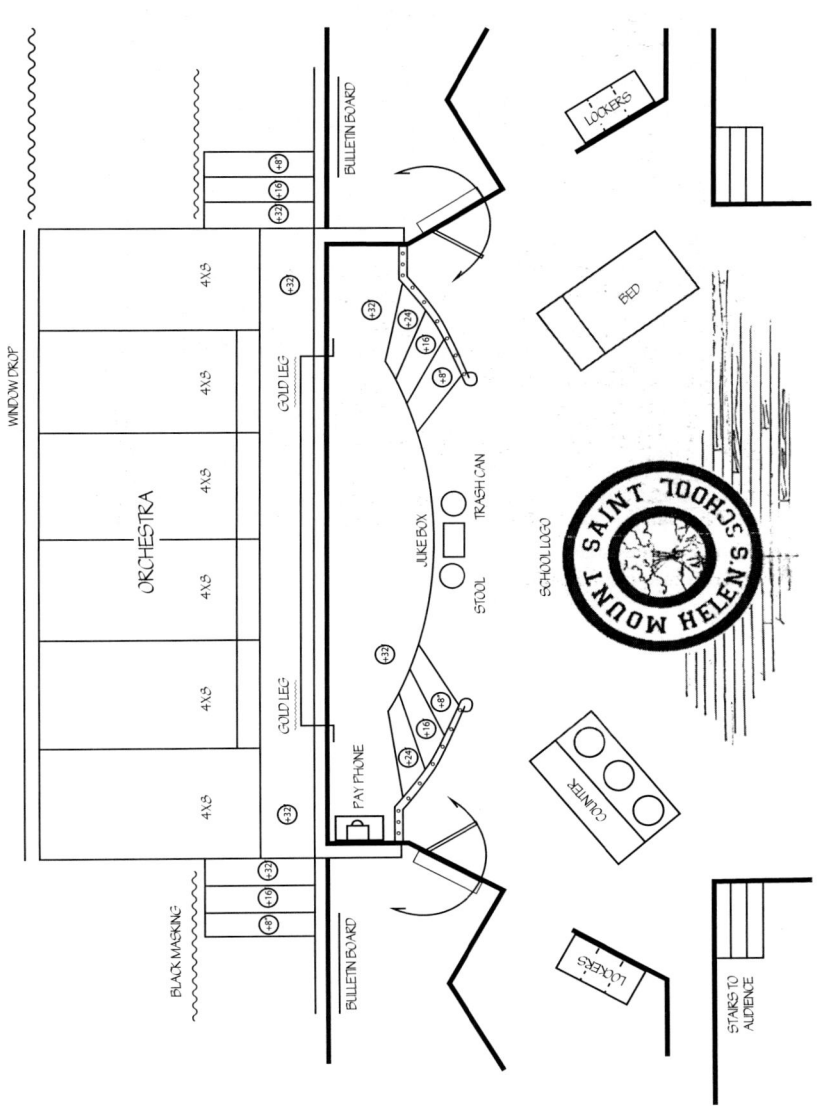

Set Design by Barry Axtell

DAN GOGGIN (Book, Music & Lyrics) came to New York from Alma, Michigan to study as a classical countertenor. He began his professional career singing in the Tony award-winning Broadway production of *Luther* starring Albert Finney. While appearing in a comic folk-duo called "The Saxons" he began writing. This led to scores for the off-Broadway musical, *Hark!* (in which he also appeared), the Broadway production of *Legend* and two revues. Goggin received the 1986 Outer Critics' Circle Awards given to *Nunsense* for Best Musical, Best Book, and Best Music. *Nunsense* and *Nunsense 2: The Second Coming*, both starring Rue McClanahan have been recorded for the A&E Television Network. *Nunsense 3: The Jamboree* toured the U.S. starring Georgia Engel and has been recorded for television at the Grand Ole Opry starring Vicki Lawrence. *Nunsense A-Men!* opened at the 47th Street Theatre in New York in June 1998 and has since been produced with *Laugh-In*'s Arte Johnson, impressionist Frank Gorshin, and Olympic Champion Greg Louganis. *Nuncrackers: The Nunsense Christmas Musical* premiered in October 1998, followed by a national tour starring Dody Goodman, Jeff Trachta and Dawn Wells. *The Nuncrackers* television special playing on the PBS network starring Rue McClanahan with guest star John Ritter, received an Emmy nomination for Best Musical Score. *Meshuggah-Nuns: The Ecumenical Nunsense* premiered in September 2002 and is currently out on DVD. The All-Star touring production of *Nunsense* featuring Kaye Ballard, Georgia Engel, Mimi Hines, Darlene Love and Lee Meriwether marked the 20th anniversary of the original show. In 2004 Dan's "serious piece" *The Traditional Latin Mass* was recorded by cast members and friends. In 2005, *Nunsensations: The Nunsense Vegas Revue* premiered, and in 2008 there was a national tour starring Sally Struthers. In 2009, *Sister Robert Anne's Cabaret Class (A one-nun musical)* and *Nunset Boulevard: The Nunsense Hollywood Bowl Show* opened. Most recently, the original *Nunsense* celebrated it's 30th Anniversary with the Mega-Nunsense version featuring a cast of 60 in the Saint Louis Muny's 11,000 seat amphitheatre. www.nunsense.com.

Rentals/Sales of Little Sisters of Hoboken nun habits, rosaries, the "dying nun Hat," the sister Mary Annette puppet, show prizes, DVDs, CDs, and gift items are available from Nunsense/Nunstuff, Route 9-D, Garrison, NY 10524. Phone: 1-800-YES-NUNS. www.nunsense.com